monsoonbooks

SOMEONE IS COMING

T. A. Morton is a Singapore
2020 she was shortlisted for the Virginia Prize for Fiction and
the Bridport Prize. She is currently completing her Masters in
Crime and Thriller Writing at Cambridge University.

'A beautifully written, gripping thriller
about history and memory and how they intersect.'
– Sophie Hannah,
Sunday Times and *New York Times* bestselling author

Someone is Coming

T. A. Morton

monsoon

monsoonbooks

First published in 2022
by Monsoon Books Ltd
www.monsoonbooks.co.uk

No.1 The Lodge, Burrough Court,
Burrough on the Hill, Melton Mowbray LE14 2QS, UK

ISBN (paperback): 9781915310040
ISBN (ebook): 9781915310057

Cover design by Cover Kitchen.

A Cataloguing-in-Publication data record is available from the British
Library.

Printed and bound in Great Britain by Clays Ltd, Elcograf S.p.A.
24 23 22   1 2 3

For Cordelia Ann

The Oral History Centre was established in 1979. We are mandated to record, preserve and disseminate the history of Singapore through oral history methodology. This is done through the interviewing of individuals who have served prominently as leaders and innovators in their field of work, as well as individuals who were eyewitnesses or participants in historical events affecting Singapore. Our interviews are made available for public consultation, subject to the agreement of interviewees.

https://www.nas.gov.sg/archivesonline/oral_history_interviews/faq

Accession Number 0003351. Reel one.

Interview with Philip Goundry. Born in Singapore 1910, son of plantation manager Gilbert Goundry. Resident of Cullodena Plantation, Kedah, 1912-1924. Home-schooled with brother Jimmy by mother, Mary Elizabeth Goundry née Mckenna. Recalls daily routines on rubber plantation. Boom and bust period. Relationship of his father with workers. Sightings of pontianak (vampire) and tiger. Ghost stories told by amah and other planters. Abandoned house on plantation, trail of leaves. Murders of plantation managers. Mother's disappearance. Red Pied Piper. Return Singapore work for R.S. Tyrone shipping, marriage, wife died. Brother Jimmy ...

Monday Morning

Chalfont St Giles, England, 2006

A door bangs.

A playful breeze.

Then stillness.

'Someone is coming,' I whisper, not expecting Michelle to hear it, but she does and looks over at me.

'Who is coming?' She is trying to find my jumper, the pale blue one I bought decades ago in Italy. I suddenly think I will never go back to Italy. I will never again sit in Sienna, sip wine, eat olives and watch the world go by. That thought makes me want to cry but I swallow it. Time must have a stop. Huxley wrote that, didn't he?

She finds my jumper and walks over to me. 'Who is coming, Philip?'

'I don't remember his name. He is coming today; that's what Tom said last night. They came to see me before, a bunch of them. I am to be interviewed.'

'Oh yes, that's right, you are. I see there is a table set up for your interview. Well, here you go, arms up,' she says.

I try and lift my arms, but they feel heavy and sore; she slips the jumper over my head and her arms circle my neck as she tries to fold down the collar of my shirt.

'We want you looking your best, don't we?'

I want to say it's a bit late for that, but I don't. She moves me forward and pulls down the jumper. I sit back and immediately feel that it hasn't gone down all the way. I don't say anything.

'Lin, isn't it? His name? Doctor Lin, that's what it says on the daily register. He's coming all the way from Singapore, isn't he?'

She is looking around for my water. I notice her nurse's blue tunic is looking snug around her belly, has she put on weight? I want to tell her that her mascara has smudged on her left eye, that it looks as if she hasn't brushed her hair since last week. She should take more pride in herself; she is relatively attractive.

She asks, 'Are you excited?'

I shrug, it hurts to shrug. 'I suppose so. I have been interviewed before; you know about my work. I was interviewed many times.'

'Oh, I know, still it's been a while.' She is right, it has been a while, probably over fifteen years. 'Still, they must be excited, interviewing you. You always spoke so lovely, like Richard Burton and the other one. Oh, what's his name? The Welsh poet that sounded a bit like Burton.'

'Dylan Thomas.'

'Ah that's it.' She grins at me. 'So why is he interviewing you again?'

'Oral history interviews, part of a government initiative to record old Singaporean history. They are trying to get around to all of us before we die and take our past with us.' I give out a little laugh that turns into a cough that I can't control.

She pats my back. 'You okay?'

I nod, gasping for air. I take a breath in. I count one, two, three and breathe out. The cough has subsided for now. 'You know I grew up in Malaya.'

'You did? Well, I had no idea. You never wrote about it, did you?'

'No, I didn't.' I look away from her. Both my nurses, Tom and Michelle, made a conscious effort to read most of what I wrote, which was kind but unnecessary. I don't like to talk now about the books I wrote, it seems so long ago, another lifetime.

'Still, you're as sharp as they come.'

I look at her surprised.

'Your memory, I don't know many people that can remember things like you, young or old.'

I smile. 'I am lucky in that way.'

'You sure are. Mind you, there are things that I would rather forget, like those nuns in the convent, I would like to forget the rings on their fingers beating down on my head.' She smiles.

'You know you can choose to forget it.'

She stands back and looks at me. 'Can you? Well, you must teach me how to do it, I'd love to forget all that, I tell you.'

'It's part of a meditation practice. I learned it in India at an ashram. You know, I now can't recall the real reason why I went there. I think I wasn't sleeping well at the time ... nightmares, sleepwalking ... someone mentioned it could help.'

There is a gentle knock on the door, a slight man looks in, he is wearing navy trousers, a white shirt and a thin black rain jacket, his hair is glistening; it looks wet. Is it raining?

'Mr Goundry?'

Michelle answers for me. 'Yes, this is Mr Goundry. I'm sure he will allow you to call him Philip.'

He smiles. 'May I come in?'

I say, 'Of course, please.'

He comes towards me and offers his hand. 'I am Doctor Lin.'

'How do you do, Doctor Lin?'

'I am well and how are you?'

'Well thank you. Won't you sit?'

Michelle points to the chair by the window. 'We set out a small table for you. Are you using a tape recorder? We thought you would be using a tape recorder.' She speaks fast as if she is nervous.

'Yes,' he nods, 'yes I am.' He sits down without taking off his coat.

'Right. Well, we thought here would be best, didn't we, Philip? The windows are double glazed so there isn't much noise, and the gardener isn't expected to arrive until Thursday, but you never know with him. But there shouldn't be anyone to disturb you.'

He nods again and smiles. 'Thank you, this is perfect. What a nice view you have.' His accent is not strong, he is well educated, I assume he probably went to university or school over here. We both look out towards the fields; the sun has come out and is beaming down on the long grass outside. I see droplets of water, glistening on the leaves of the small roses that stand right against my window. I didn't realise it was raining.

'Typical English weather,' he says and lets out a chuckle, placing his hand over his mouth as if to conceal his smile.

'Yes, I suppose it is. Have you been in the UK long?'

'A month, mostly in the British archives in London.

'Oh yes?'

'Yes, just looking through some photographs and other things.' He doesn't look at me.

'I see.'

He turns and faces me. 'Thank you so much for agreeing

to do this. It is a great honour for us to interview you.'

I smile. 'Of course, I am glad to contribute my account of growing up in Malaya.'

I say that and regret it, it sounds so formal, so pretentious; I can almost detect Michelle's eyes rolling.

He places a large heavy black bag on the floor; he opens it and lifts out a tape recorder placing it on the table. It looks old like it is from another time. He then takes out two small microphones with long wires.

'So, I'll be off to do my rounds. I'll bring some tea in an hour. If there is anything, please just use the rope.' Michelle points to the blue rope that is hanging in the centre of the room. 'I'll close the door behind me.'

He nods at her and looks at me. 'Have you been here long?'

'Five months. I fell at home, and they thought it would be for the best.'

'It is a nice place.'

'Yes, yes, it is. Everyone is very nice.'

I cough and lean forward; I suddenly feel a sense of dread that all of this is going to end badly. That I shouldn't do this. To be honest when they first showed up I hadn't seen anyone for months. I don't get many visitors anymore. No one writes, no one calls, that is the downside of living to an old age, you outlive everyone. Anyway, I agreed probably too quickly. I didn't think it through. I said, yes would be happy to. They said they would send someone to talk to me, someone to record my memories. Ego got the better of me. I thought I had done my best to kill it off, but it rises again like an unwanted thought. I told them that my mind is as fresh as a daisy, my memories as clear as yesterday.

I lied; my mind is waterlogged, sometimes I can recall snippets, they come and go like violent rainstorms in the jungle.

I'm so old now, I don't even sound like myself. My granddaughter told me last Christmas; you are ancient like the pharaohs. The pharaohs. Slave owners. I look down at my hands, protruding blue lines, dark spots.

Time must have a stop. Time must have a stop, was that the title of the book? Or was it a line? I can't remember. I'm sure it was Huxley. He taught Orwell, or was it the other way around?

I breathe out and he looks up.

'Sorry, just need to make sure everything is working.' He is plugging in the microphones; he speaks into one. 'Testing, one, two.' He stops and rewinds, his voice sounds, 'Testing, one, two.'

I start to shift in my seat. I'm getting anxious, I feel as if I made a promise to someone a long time ago not to talk of the jungle. I am about to say I'm sorry, I can't, I don't feel well, when he sits up.

'Interview with Mr Philip Goundry. Accession Number

3351. Reel One. So, Mr Goundry, we are here to discuss your childhood and what it was like to grow up on a Cullodena Plantation in the early part of the twentieth century. Could you first describe the house you lived in?'

'Umm, sure,' I move again and start to speak softly, 'it was a five-bedroom bungalow.'

He moves the microphone closer to me. I clear my throat and speak louder.

'It was a nice big house. Beautiful flower garden filled with orchids, mango and banana trees. My brother, Jimmy, and I had our own rooms. I remember the first floor was mostly wooden, timber. There was a wide staircase. We had a large veranda that wrapped around the entire house, typical Malayan style.'

I laugh. 'I remember the glass on the windows had a strange green tint that made everything glow in the evenings. The servants would take down the chik blinds when the storms came, or the sun beamed in. We didn't have much, but my mother loved to paint. You know she painted all the phases of the moon on our bedroom walls.' I smile. 'She would tell us about her home, people living in cities, so many people. She would tell us about the cold icy North Sea and the wind that tried to get into your bones.'

'Where did you mother come from?'

'Scotland, well Edinburgh, like my father. They often spoke about home.' I look down, I try to see their faces, but

I can't.

'I remember feeling a bit jealous that I didn't really know what home was; I didn't know the people they talked about, the streets they mentioned. It was like my parents shared a secret place that I would never know. It is funny now; it was as if the whole world was existing outside of where we were.'

I stop and look towards the door, expecting one of them to walk in but they don't, everything is quiet. I continue. 'My parents had two cooks, a gardener and of course our amah.' I clear my throat again.

'The house wasn't as fancy as some of the other plantation bungalows. My father had bought the plantation cheap, and the house I believe was built just a few years before. It was wooden with a palm-thatched roof that was changed every year as I recall. My father did not approve of the other plantation houses that were too fine, this wasn't our country he would often say. The others don't remember that. I remember when I was very small, Jimmy and I shared a room but, as he was that bit older than me, he moved into his own room later. I remember one night we found a scorpion on his pillow.'

'Did it sting him?'

'No but Amah was very frightened. She said the devil was in the house and we would need to be careful.'

He laughs, 'I see.'

'We decided the next day to make scorpion catchers with

the latex from the trees. Amah would change his sheets every night and then bless the room, whisper her prayers and mantras and light candles.'

'That must have been quite scary for your brother.'

'No, he loved it, standing there watching her, like a precious prince. I would roll my eyes and stick out my tongue at him.' I laugh. 'Once I captured a scorpion and was going to drop it in his bed as a joke but one of my dad's workers saw me. He told me to be careful, that scorpions could kill children.'

I'm rambling now, I'm nervous. 'One of my earliest memories was of fires, small fires outside.'

'Fires?'

'Yes, left over from the burning of the jungle. Slash and burn, it was a method they used to make way for the rubber trees to be planted. There were many animals too, bats, beetles the size of your hand. Monkeys, herds of elephants that could easily destroy acres of rubber trees if they wanted. Huge frogs, toads and fireflies. Crickets that chirped the whole night through. My father had designed a bridge close by, that is why I think we moved there. My father trained as an engineer but grew bored and decided to go into the rubber trade. There was a lot of money to be made then and so I assume he wanted in on it.' I laugh. 'I don't know that for sure, but I think that is what he wanted. So, they bought a rubber plantation and settled into life. They were good at it.'

I picture them in the front room, a book filled with numbers. My mother laughing. 'They were a good team. My father was well respected and well liked not just by the other planters but by the locals and the workers. You see he respected everyone, including the jungle, he always said that we were at the mercy of the jungle and all its allies.'

'Who were the jungle's allies?'

'The animals, insects, the wind, and sun, all things that man could not control. He said we were always at the mercy of the jungle, that it could come back and reclaim its land anytime.' I laugh. 'As a child I always thought the jungle was a god, and all the small statues and prayers that the locals said were to appease him.'

'An angry god?'

'Yes, well not always but my father always told us never to ask too much of it. There was a great fire when I was about four or five. It wasn't planned and it raged throughout the jungle for days, destroying everything. The tappers tried to protect the trees but a lot of them were damaged. But that's the funny thing about the jungle, it recovers quickly. There was an old house in the middle of our plantation that used to be the main house but had been abandoned. Half of it had burnt down; the rest was left intact. Our Chinese amah used to say in her market Malay, Ini rumah tak begitu baik.'

'This house is not good. Why did she say that?'

'She said there was a demon that lived in the house, that the demon had stopped the fire from destroying it.' I swallow, I don't know why I said that. I shouldn't have mentioned it.

'Do you know the history of that house?'

I look towards the floor. 'No, I don't I'm afraid. No, hold on … something about a death. A young woman hung herself or something. Well, maybe Amah told us that to make sure we kept away from the house; after the fire it was left in a terrible state. She said if we went close to it a young woman would come and get us; that she was a demon and she would take over our bodies and our souls would die.' I laugh. 'It's ridiculous what adults tell young children to scare them into staying away from places.'

Suddenly I see a girl, orchids on the ground, the girl pointing. Something was wrong. I was scared, where was Jimmy? I shake my head and try to ignore it.

'Did you ever see anything strange by the house?' He asks that softly; I look at him surprised.

'What do you mean?' I swallow, trying to suppress that vision.

He smiles at me. 'There are many Malayan ghost stories and legends. I just wondered whether you thought it was haunted?'

'Well, to be honest, the whole jungle feels haunted with strange sounds, hidden spaces in the daylight perfect for concealing bad deeds. Cries of unknown animals; voices that can be heard but there is no one there, no one you can see. The jungle is probably the scariest place in the world.'

'Especially for a child?'

'Yes, well, not when you grow up in it. I knew it was more powerful than me, that there was a reason that my amah prayed to the gods of the jungle to protect us.'

He nods. 'So, you learned Malay?'

'Yes, I did. I'm afraid I don't remember much of it. Back them my accent was as thick as my mother and father's; Scottish with traces of Malay.'

'Could you take me through a normal day on the plantation? For your father, I mean.'

'Well, he was up early around five thirty. There was a roll call with the workers at six and then morning tea. He came back around ten just after our first lesson and we had a big breakfast together. He then left again and went to the field from eleven to two o'clock. He went to all the different fields to check up on everything. Then he would return, have tiffin and go out again till six. After that he would come home, wash and then sit on the veranda at the back in his sarong, drink sundowners and smoke. We were never allowed to sit with him then; it was his time to relax. We would then have dinner and after that my parents would play cards and read. Jimmy and I would be sent to bed. On the weekends they would go to the club and see friends.'

I laugh, 'I remember they would often bring people back to our house afterwards. They would drink more, someone would always sing and they would dance, you know, have a hoolie.'

'A hoolie?'

'Yes, a hoolie. It's like a spur-of-the-moment party where people dance, sing, play instruments. I remember one of my father's friends played the flute and they would all dance around.' I laugh. 'Jimmy and I would wake up and join in. One night we danced until the sun came up. I remember my father went straight out on his inspection.'

'Did you ever go out with your father on his inspections?'

'Yes, on most days after school we were able to join my father on his afternoon inspections. We used to ride our bicycles up and down the dirt roads. Often, we would follow and watch him talk to his assistant while he checked the tapping, the trees. The thick latex streamed down the trees like thick blood, it's flow slow, almost hypnotic. I liked to touch the markings made by the chisels, feel the man-made groove alongside the natural bark, every one of them was different, some smooth, some rough, it depended on how sharp their chisels were.'

Doctor Lin grins at me. 'You were very lucky.'

'I suppose I was.' I smile politely. I swallow some water and look at Doctor Lin. I suddenly remember my father furious, his face red. He threatened my mother with his fist. Her face was still, her expression undisturbed as if he wasn't there. It was something about those sacks in the workers quarters. She told him to get rid of them. Memories don't spring up too often with me, they have submerged like the deep cuts into the trees. Overgrown, their marks still lie underneath, scars that I avoided. I had forgotten I carried them. Someone at the ashram told me memories can only lie dormant for so long. Be careful Philip. I shake out my head. He hasn't noticed.

'What about school?'

'My parents didn't like the look of the local school and so my mother decided to home school. We were meant to go back to Scotland, well that was always the plan. Materials were sent over from the UK. My mother had worked for a few years as a schoolteacher in Scotland, she loved teaching us. I think Jimmy and I were very lucky to be able to stay home with them; most of the other children were sent away. We got along very well, Jimmy and I, well I suppose we had to.' I laugh.

He nods. 'Did you miss seeing other children?'

'Umm, no, not really, you don't miss what you don't know. There were some local children we played with sometimes but for the most we spent time by ourselves. The other western children considered us outcasts. Even though we were invited to birthday parties they looked upon us as if we were locals.

Jimmy's skin was dark, he looked more like a local; I took after my mother, I freckled easily, my skin pale. Jimmy was a bit older than me.'

'Yes, you said. What was the age difference?'

'Four years. We got along well though. He was protective but not overly. Sometimes if we entered part of the jungle that we didn't know well, he made sure he always stood in front. If we played games, he would never let me win but he would always try and encourage me to do better.' I suddenly see him sitting at his desk writing frantically, *Go away Philip! Get out. I must finish this before they come back. Stop looking! GO!* I shake out my head again hoping Doctor Lin hasn't noticed. He hasn't. I give him a timid smile.

'Did you go to church?'

'No, never. My father didn't believe in God.'

'And your mother?'

'I don't know about her. I can't remember, but it never came up.' I try and recall whether she did say anything about god, she never did. 'I didn't learn about Jesus until I went to school.'

'What about the locals? Did you father have a problem when they worshipped their gods?'

'No, he didn't, he didn't mind them setting up their shrines. To be honest he was pretty accommodating to them and if a local bomoh said that we shouldn't plant or disturb land in a particular spot my father would always listen to him. That's funny isn't it, that he believed in the bomoh more than the western Christian god.'

He doesn't respond. 'Do you know when your father and mother came over to the Federated Malay Straits?'

'No, no I don't. I know they met and were married very quickly, and my mother came out with him on the steamer. It wasn't easy for a lot of women to be out there. You know with the heat and isolation, electricity only arrived for a few hours in the evenings if we were lucky. She didn't have many friends, well to be honest there was no one for her to be friends with. She played cards mostly with my father's friends or the other western men that came to the house. She liked playing cards, she was very good at them. She also sewed, she loved making clothes. Actually, she often complained that someone was stealing her clothes.'

'Stealing them?' He looks up.

'Yes, she would make things and the next day she couldn't find them.'

'Was it the servants?'

'I presume.' I swallow again and hold my breath. Orange, burnt-red orange, blood-orange fabric. Women's underwear on brown hairy legs. I suddenly cough.

'Are you okay?'

'Yes. Water, water.' He passes it to me, and I take it; my

29

hands shaking. I don't know what is happening, why my mind is allowing images like this to start coming through. Be careful, Philip. I don't want to indulge them. I am not the sort of person that likes to reminisce. I gulp, that feeling of dread has started to rise again. This was a mistake, this whole thing, I should never have agreed to it, to him. People say we should let things go, set them free but you can't set free those things that made you, you can only allow them not to overtake you. But no, I can't end it like this, I am after all Philip Goundry, I still have a reputation and legacy to protect. I clear my throat and decide to speak again.

'During that time, tigers were a nuisance; they killed the livestock and the odd tapper if they fell asleep outside. I remember there was one tiger that started becoming a bit more familiar with us, she started to come closer to our bungalow. One evening my father saw her from our veranda and instead of shooting her he whispered for us to come out. We all came out and watched the tiger walk across our garden, she stopped and lay down under our old mango tree.'

'Did she know you were there?'

'Yes, she looked over at us and we looked at her, she lay there for a while and closed her eyes. My mother and brother went into the house and my father and I just sat mesmerised. He never said anything to me as we sat there. We just breathed in and out as quiet as we could, waiting for the tiger to make a move, but she never did. God, when I think about it now my father didn't even have a gun handy. We sat there until we were called in to dinner. We ate fast but by the time we came back out, she was gone. I remember a few months later there was an incident with the tiger. I don't know if it was the same tiger, but we had a cat, a rather pathetic small ginger thing, given to us for Christmas. Anyway, one morning we awoke to Amah's screaming. Our cat had been mauled, its small, lifeless body left on the front steps. She believed that the tiger had done it. Amah said it was a very bad sign.'

'Do you know why?'

'Tigers were sacred and normally stayed away from humans. For one of them to commit an act like that was a sign that something was very wrong, that someone in our house was committing a very bad sin. Amah said the tiger was warning us to stop and if we didn't she would punish us further.' Hairy legs with white bloomers, a green dress, she stands behind him buttoning up the back. I shut my eyes fast.

'I need a rest,' I suddenly say.

This catches him off guard and he mumbles, 'Sorry, of course.' He stands up and turns off the recording. 'I will give you some space.' He leaves the room, I stare at his jacket on the chair, one of the arms is dangling, it is almost hitting the floor. I sit back and sigh. Hairy legs and women's underwear. I want to laugh but I don't, what a strange image, but I shouldn't go there. Be careful, Phillip. I shouldn't go further, I'm afraid what is on the other side.

Michelle enters. 'Are you alright there, Philip?'

'Yes.' I reply weakly.

'Are you not well?'

'I'm fine,' I say, 'just tired. So many questions he asked. It was almost too much.'

'It always is, like opening an old can of worms,' she says. 'You have to be careful sometimes, you don't know what you will get.'

'I had a good life.' I grab her arm as she reaches for the empty glass next to me.

'No doubt,' she answers me, 'but there is always something, isn't there? We all have those skeletons in our closets, don't we? Even if we don't want to acknowledge them.'

I don't reply and let go of her arm, my eyes follow her as she moves around my room setting up the table for lunch. 'I don't know whether I am doing the right thing talking to him.'

She looks at me confused. 'Well, that's for you to decide isn't it. Sometimes it does no good looking back, it only opens up old scars.'

I nod, the way she says it reminds me of my mother and I want to cry but I don't.

'He is joining you for lunch, isn't he?'

I nod. 'Yes, I think so.'

'It is fish, white cod with new potatoes and carrots followed by the chocolate cake you like, let me see if I can get you an extra piece, okay?' She hands me the word search book I am working through, the doctor told me it was a good way to train the brain. I hated them to start with but now I am addicted to them.

She walks towards the door, and I say, 'Maybe a glass of wine?'

She laughs. 'Ahh you're not that bad, I see. Maybe this evening.'

She leaves and I open the book. It falls on a page titled 'Types of Monkeys'. I pick up my pen and let my eyes try and decipher a clear word. I see 'gibbons' top right corner downwards. I mark it. I remember their distant call in the jungle, they stayed away from us, they knew something wasn't right, animals have that instinct, they don't question it like we do, they stay away when they feel it is dangerous.

Monday Afternoon

The afternoon is easier. I talk a lot. Sometimes I think I am boring him, but he smiles off and on. He has lunch with me. Sitting opposite he eats the fish and potatoes they gave us. It's the first time I have sat opposite anyone in a long time, it's like being in a restaurant. He doesn't seem to mind as I cough a little, as my hand starts to shake when he fills my water glass too full. We speak about his trip over here, how long he is staying, who else he is going to see. He is heading to the archives tomorrow, The British Archives to search for things about my father. I nod and say I wish I could join him; I really do wish I could join him. We eat chocolate cake and custard for dessert, there is skin at the top of the custard. I notice he doesn't remove it to the side like I do but mixes it into the cake. He will be here a month interviewing, researching, he is trying to locate the old maps detailing the position of all the old plantations. I tell him I can locate ours and he nods appreciatively. That would be great. He says he will hopefully find the map and bring it by during the next few interviews, there will be approximately four in total, each lasting two hours.

'They will be edited down,' he tells me, 'just to remove coughs, laughter and whether we talk about things that aren't relevant.'

I nod and say, 'I appreciate the attention.'

He says, 'Why, of course. We are honoured you agreed to speak to us.' I watch his eyes scan the room.

'All I have is books I'm afraid and that old TV.'

He asks me, 'You have no children to look after you?'

It doesn't offend me, sometimes people say things without thinking. 'I have a son. He lives in Scotland with his family.'

'Your wife?'

'She died when I was thirty-seven, she was twenty-five.'

'Oh, I'm so sorry,' he says softly.

'An accident,' I say. I tap my fingers on the table and decide not to meet his eyes.

'You never married again?'

I shake my head and I don't answer. He waits for me to expand; I don't, and he doesn't ask anything more.

They come and clear away our plates and leave us a pot of tea. He takes his weak with lots of milk and sugar, I take mine strong and black.

He starts the recording again. 'Interview with Mr Philip Goundry. Accession number 3351. Reel One. Mr Philip, can we talk about the area where you lived? How many plantations were there around yours?'

'Five, I think, yes, five. I can't recall the names'

'So, the whole area was rubber plantations?'

I smile. 'Yes, pretty much. There were some smaller ones, but they were owned by the Chinese. All the plantations led onto a main road and to a small town. We had a club with a tennis court, a shop, post office, cricket pitch and church. It was as similar to a small English town as you can imagine, except for the heat. Oh, and the smell of rubber, that was also unique. Everyone was very friendly; my parents were friends with the managers and their families from other plantations.'

Doctor Lin nods, adjusting the sound on the tape recorder. 'So let me see if I can remember some names. Charlie Walsh, Herbert Scales, Geoffrey Gallagher, and Campbell something. Sorry, I can't remember his name.'

'And they lived in the plantations surrounding yours?'

I nod. 'Yes. Yes they did. They were all quite young as I remember, none of them had children then. We saw them a lot, they were almost like family, well at one stage. People moved on a lot back then, they either got better jobs, or saved up enough and went home. I guess that was hard for my parents, having friends and then letting them go.'

He nods.

* * *

I tell Michelle later that we didn't discuss too much today, we only spoke about problems with the workers, the price of rubber and the heat. I say to Michelle that it is good to talk about the past, to really remember things.

She smiles and replies, 'That is great, Philip.' She hands me my tablets. Two blue, one pink.

'You're as right as rain,' she says.

I have lived a life, I think, before I sleep. A very good life. I am lucky, I think, as I drift off.

Monday evening

In the middle of the night, I waken suddenly. Heavy breathing, someone is in the room with me, someone is standing in the corner, they are watching me. I am afraid. I go to cry out, but I can't. I can't speak and then I feel someone pressing down on my chest, like they are sitting on top of me, my heart starts to beat furiously, and I gasp. I can't move my arms, but my legs are beating against the mattress. I hear the words, *tarik nafas, tarik nafas*. My door is shut but I see a line of light along the crack. Then it suddenly stops and I'm free; the presence is gone, and I can move again. I sit up and call the duty nurse.

It is Tom, he rushes in, 'You okay?'

'No. No, I had a nightmare.'

He switches on the light and looks at me, his head immediately retracts, and his eyes open wide.

'What? What is it?' I ask.

'Your face, the scratches.'

'What?'

He hands me my shaving mirror. I look into it and see deep scratches lining my cheek, like claw marks from a young tiger cub. What is this? I start to cry. I know it's foolish, but I say to him, 'I didn't do this, I couldn't. Look at my hands.' I lift them up and show him. My nails are dark underneath. Blood, fresh blood, deep scratches. 'Why, why would I do this?' I sob.

He rubs my back and tells me he's going to get me something to calm me down. He brings in a syringe and injects me. I don't ask what it is. He whispers, 'Something to help you settle.' He sits with me.

'I have never done anything like this before,' I say and he smiles gently at me.

'Don't worry, don't worry, you must have had a bad dream.' He sits and asks about Doctor Lin. I tell him what I said. Childhood memories about growing up on a plantation and how my father taught us to shoot as youngsters, to kill snakes and other animals such as tigers.

'Did you ever see a tiger?' he asks

'Yes, a few times, but I kept still, I could never shoot anything so beautiful.'

'Maybe that is what has gotten to you.'

'What?'

'Talking about the past. That can do it sometimes, reawakening all the old memories. Makes you think about things you haven't thought about in a while.'

I nod. 'But I had a good childhood,' I say.

'Well then maybe it was the chicken they served at dinner.' I laugh loudly and start coughing. He helps me sit up and gives me some water. I lie down again and feel exhausted.

'Getting old isn't for wimps,' I say.

He laughs. 'Try and sleep.'

I can feel a certain coolness circulating throughout my veins. My eyelids become heavy. My mind shuts off and I'm in the dark, safe, with my mother. She is humming and then suddenly she is gone and I'm alone in a room, crying; someone is trying to open the door, someone I'm afraid of. *Tarik nafas. Tarik nafas.*

Tuesday Morning

I waken, it is morning. I hear a vacuum cleaner in the hallway and one of the nurses giggling. I roll over and look at the clock, it is eleven thirty.

Michelle pops her head in. 'There you are, Philip, I was beginning to worry about you, that was some sort of sleep you had there.'

I clear my throat, it is dry. 'I had a bad dream.'

'So I heard. Tom gave you something didn't he, it sure did the job.'

'Yes, yes it did.'

'You feeling better?'

'Yes, I think so.'

'Good, I'll leave you to get changed.'

I sit up and rotate to the side of the bed. I look at my clothes in the corner, all neatly folded in the order I put them on, underwear, socks, trousers and shirt. Then I see my watch to the side, and I give out a sudden gasp, the watch, a leather watch strap, my father's? On the corner table in the kitchen. He always took it off when he entered the house. Time plays no role in my house; he used to say like it meant something important. My mother at the table, peeling, washing, sewing, she grins up at him grateful that he has returned safe from his inspection. These are dangerous times she'd tell us; we all need to be on our guard. Dangerous times, why were they dangerous?

I walk over to my clothes, remembering her stitching my father's shirt back together after it ripped on a rose bush that was dying. It had been one of their wedding presents; pink roses that had survived the trip out there but due to heat the roses had started to suffer in the jungle. She had loved roses, she had loved … and then I stop. I remember, she left the plantation, one day she was gone, vanished, she never came back. I sit down on the floor in my pyjamas and stare at the swirls on the carpet. She left when I was young, when my brother was a bit older. How could I not remember that? How odd the mind is to black that out, my sadness, our loss. I haven't thought about her for years.

Michelle walks in. 'Are you okay down there?' She comes towards me.

'Yes,' I say, my eyes not leaving the carpet. 'Yes.' I blink through tears.

'Come on then let me help you up.' I stand up and look at her. She sees my tears.

'Are you alright?'

I sniff. 'Yes, I'm fine, just stupid thoughts.'

'Memories?'

'Yes,' she hands me a tissue, 'how did you know?'

'Tom. He mentioned it in last night's notes. It's that man, Doctor Lin, that has come to interview you about your past.'

'I don't know, I'm so confused. I just remembered my mother left when I was a child, she vanished, we never saw her again. I blocked it out.'

'What do you mean you blocked it out?'

'I didn't remember.'

'Ahh sure don't be worrying about that now. We all do what we must to get by.'

'But I didn't remember.'

'I know but you remember now, and sure she wouldn't want you to be getting all upset about it, it was a long time ago.'

'It was.' I nod.

'Don't worry about it. They are serving bread and butter pudding today; you like that don't you?'

I nod.

'I'll ask whether they can give you an extra portion of custard. Would you like that? I know you love your custard.'

'I do.'

'Good, well there you go; you do the rest alright?'

'Yes. Thank you.'

She leaves me and I look out into the small garden I have.

I see roses, pale pink roses, small ones, tea roses, not like the ones she had. They dance in the wind. It is a summer's day, the sky is bluer than it has been for years I think, I can't be sure. I suppose I never took the time to really look at the sky, not since I was a child.

* * *

Do you think that is possible to forget something as big as that? I bet you don't. And believe me I wouldn't have thought it possible either. Sometimes people asked me about my family, I would say they are dead and that was enough for them to stop. No one asked further and for those times when memories seeped through I would count down from a hundred and wait for the tiger to appear. I learned how to do it in India. My teacher said, if I show you this you will have to deny yourself the truth, it's as if you were to sign a deal with the devil. He said you must be careful, Philip; if those memories come up they can destroy you. I said I didn't care.

Breathe out, one hundred, ninety-nine, ninety-eight … three, two, one and the tiger would walk towards me; once it reached me it would lick my face. My own memories evaporated behind the tiger's swinging tail. I began to forget why I needed the tiger and over time the tiger did not come at all.

I grab a pen and an old notebook out of the small box of my prized possessions that I had taken with me. I sit at my old desk that I haven't sat at in a month. It is to be donated to a society upon my death. My old desk feels the same. I look at the pen, it is a thin biro and it slides out of my hands as I try to grip it. I pick it up and stare at the blank page. Words used to come so easy, stories of young men fighting in the war, stories that were considered a classic, stories that I couldn't stop writing. All those young men, their lives. I tried to recall everything I had heard them say, what they wanted and why they were here with me in the trenches. It became my life's work writing these novels, fiction they said but they weren't, every one of them was based on someone that I had met and spoken to.

A clean fresh piece of paper. I squint and breathe out, maybe the past will come through my fingers better than my head. I start to write.

My mother liked Herbert Scales, he was tall, thin and elegant. I suppose now she looked upon him as if she was in love, there was a flirtation. No one likes to see their mother flirt. My father enjoyed Herbert being around, they seemed happy the three of them, it was as if Herbert was our uncle.

I look up, was he our uncle? I can't remember.

Memory is a funny thing. Once you start to think back to a time and remember conversations, you can start to recall other

45

smaller things like smells, clothes, crates of bananas, a thick red beard turning white and long nose hair. Memories start to lay themselves out and it's up to you to place them upright on a table; you start to manoeuvre them, make sense of the puzzle. I guess that is what my brother tried to do by making lists, by writing down what people said, by arranging names, dates and events, puzzle pieces, an odd assortment of shapes, that would lead to the truth. But what truth? What was it he was searching for?

Quick, Philip! Hide it! Someone is coming.

Now memories come thick and heavy like the rains that fall in the jungle. Dense droplets filled with water washing the leaves and soaking into the ground, cleansing the acrid smell of rubber, cleansing the jungle of its sins. People believed that the jungle was its own entity, they did spells, made sacrifices to the gods of the jungles to allow them to build and plant crops, crops that were plentiful that did not disturb the jungle too much.

My mother standing waiting, her red dress that had now faded, burnt in the sun, to more of a blood orange. She wore it on Fridays. I remember her complaining about her undergarments that she had just received that had gone missing, stolen by the workers she guessed or the staff. She complained to my father, but he did little about it. Why would the workers want women's undergarments? Don't be silly. It did upset her, she mentioned it every evening towards the end of the meal. One night my father grew so furious he slammed down his glass and it broke, he stood up and walked out, he didn't return until the morning. My father would disappear towards the workers' quarters; they would play cards, drink, gamble. Her clothes in the suitcase, some of them missing. The burnt orange and the green silk dresses.

We sat around a wooden glossy dining table, covered in an old lace tablecloth that was too small for it. Candles, soft lights and small wine glasses filled with whisky. A gramophone in the corner, a gift from Herbert, soft sounds, wailing voices that I hated. I covered my ears with my hands and ran out of the room. They laughed. My mother in her room reading through a letter, she hides it underneath her pillow, I go in search for it later but it is gone. Another letter, tears on the veranda. My father upset. A death, a relative I never met, someone that meant something to them both.

Hide and seek, covered in leaves and dirt I shiver and giggle, he finds me, Jimmy. He looks beyond me to the abandoned house, he stares at it for a while, what is it?

Nothing, I thought I saw something.

What? What did you see?

He shakes his head.

Please tell me.

A girl and a large woman.

Maybe it is the pontianak?

He laughs, you need to stop believing in such things. They aren't true.

Amah says they are.

They are for them, for the people that live here but not for us.

But we are from here.

No, he helps me stand up, no we aren't, this isn't our home.

A whistle, our father smiling, tiffin, come on you two.

* * *

'Philip, what are you doing?'

I jump and see Michelle looking confused. 'Oh, just thought I would try and write a bit, you know, see if it could help to unlock some memories.'

'I see.' She bends over and looks at my writing.

'My handwriting is awful, always has been.'

'I see. Do you think that is a good idea?'

'Yes, I think so. It is the only thing that will help unlock my mind. Of course, I was a much better typist. I used to love the sound of the keys as I pressed down on them, it was like I was playing a symphony just for myself.' I smile.

'You have said that before.'

I nod. 'Yes, I have said that many times, the sound of the

keys. Maybe I should get a typewriter, perhaps that might help, the keys, they might help.'

She doesn't answer me, she walks around the room switching on the table lamps.

'Don't you want the TV on?'

'No thank you. I will keep at this for a bit longer.'

'Are you sure? They are showing one of yours tonight.'

'Oh no, I don't want to see that, had enough of all of that.'

'Well, if you're sure.'

'I am. Thank you, Michelle.' I nod at her and she leaves the room. I return to the page.

Wednesday Morning

'Interview with Mr Philip Goundry. Accession number 3351. Reel One. So, Mr Philip, you mentioned that your father was an engineer?'

'Yes, when they first moved out he went to work with the government but there had been some falling out. The rubber market was booming, and someone offered him the plantation at a good price, so my parents moved out to Kedah and started a new life. They met on a P&O steamer on the way out to Singapore.'

'They did? I thought they met and were married before they left Scotland.'

'Oh, did I say that? Hmm, I don't recall now.' I laugh.

'Well, I remember hearing about the trip over, how they were in second-class compartments and ate their meals together. My mother was heading to Singapore to work as a teacher in one of the convents. She was brave my mother, far braver than my father.'

'I see.' He marks down something on a pad of paper. I never noticed that before, has he marked down other things? 'What were your parents like?'

'My mother was petite, thin. She had great blue-grey eyes and long red hair, she was quite a looker, especially in the jungle. But she was tough; she worked hard and enjoyed being there; unlike the rest of the women, she loved the heat, being warm. On nights when we complained of the heat, she would tell us how cold it was where she had grown up. How the snow fell thick and that although it was beautiful, it was dangerous. She had gone out as a child and placed her hands in the thick of it and had got frostbite. We didn't know what that was. The cold, she said, it bites you like a tiger. But it won't let go and you can't shoot it, it stays there surrounds you, tries to get into your soul, in here and then it tries to destroy you, takes you all the way down to its freezing temperature. We are lucky here, no cold days, when I was a girl I never knew that places like this existed. You are very lucky both of you.' I look off for a moment, I can suddenly smell her, sweet and warm.

'Your mother sounds like an extraordinary woman.'

I nod. 'She was.' She kisses me good night, now remember Philip, someone is coming. You have to be ready. Who was coming? I don't remember. I feel tears and swallow, try and cough them out. Doctor Lin looks away embarrassed. 'They were a good team, my parents.'

He nods.

'My father was tall, stocky; he looked like a farmer; you know, well built. He tanned easily; he had the best laugh.

You could hear it for miles around, loud, deep, I think it even quietened the gibbons at the end of our garden once.'

'You had gibbons?'

'Yes, we did but my father got rid of them, they kept us up all night and in the dawn that is when they started their calls. My father went out one day with his gun and tried to shoot at them.' I laugh.

'My mother stood close to him. I think that is one of my first memories. Him standing in his underclothes and my mother in her nightdress, her hair down, trying to calm him. I used to shout at them as a child, tell them to be quiet.'

'How did your father get rid of them?'

'Slash and burn. The gibbons moved up towards the mountains, we could still hear them at night but they weren't as loud.'

My left hand is starting to shake, I grab hold of it. I don't want him to see it. It hasn't done it before; it is a new thing that has just arrived; like my dreams cloudy and dark but someone is there, someone is watching me, someone is coming. I hear my father's voice in the night and I jolt awake. I haven't heard the voice of my father for years. I lie awake and for a moment believe that I am just a boy again and my father and mother are sleeping in the next room. But then I hear Michelle out in the hallway on the phone. I hear her footsteps as she moves from room to room, and I remember that I am old, as old as the pharaohs my great granddaughter says. Pharaohs, they had slaves, built great pyramids in their own honour, worshipped dark gods and died. There was that movie, *The Ten Commandments*, Charlton Heston and Yul Brunner, great words spoken by real actors with strong voices. Men are equal, not slaved, God send a warning. The Nile turns red with blood, the plague, a green fog that gently meanders through the town searching for the firstborn to be killed. Someone is coming. The blood marks on their door, they are saved, but not the pharaoh, he loses his child; a price to pay for him not worshipping the correct god.

'How was the rubber trade when you were living there?'

'I'm not sure. I know we did go through a pretty rough period as the rubber market started to fall, it was very turbulent. But the market would go down and then up again. I do remember the front door knocking often; it was normally young men searching for work. They had been let go of, and I don't mean local men like Malay or Tamil men, I mean Europeans, white burly men, starving and desperate. If my father wasn't home my mother would feed them and send them on their way. If he was at home he would walk them back towards the gate. I suppose telling them he would put in a good word for them and that if they were still here when things picked up again they should come and see him. There were some rough times. I remember my father got involved with one of his friends in some other business. I can't recall what it was but he did come home one evening with cash.'

I swallow, seeing my mother in the front room, what did you do to get this? Get it out of the house it will only bring bad luck. My father picking me up, I will do no such thing, will I Philip? I shake my head and return to Doctor Lin. I clear my throat.

'I remember my father let go of a young Dutch man and someone had said he was seen begging outside Raffles Hotel in Singapore. Funny, isn't it?'

'Yes, yes it is. Do you recall how things were regulated?'

'Mostly through the manager and then off through to customs I assume, I'm not sure. I know our rubber was sent away to Singapore and then onwards throughout the world. It was like any other time when it was great it was great and when it was bad it was very bad. But I suppose I never felt it as a child; we always had food, a roof over our heads. Perhaps my parents kept it from me, you know how often parents withhold things that they think would upset their children.'

'Do you remember the name of the plantation next to you?'

'Um, no, it was a local Melag something, apologies. I can't remember.'

'There was a shooting there when you lived there.'

'There was? I don't remember.'

'Can you remember them? The family that lived there?'

'No, I was too young. Umm ... no actually ...'

Why, Philip, how you have grown. His face brown, his hair slick, he bends down and touches my shoulder, look at you. You don't remember me, do you?

'He was nice, the man. I think the wife remarried, she remarried the best friend of the man shot, there was some gossip about them but they moved away in the end. Campbell, I think that was his name.'

'Yes, yes it was. John Campbell.'

I nod. There is a silence, he looks down again at his pad.

'Did your parents ever meet Somerset Maugham on his travels out there?'

'My father did, I believe, well he was at the club one night when he was there.'

'Did he speak to him?

'I don't know, he did say he was a very shy man, it surprised him. My parents loved Maugham though, they had most of his books before he came to stay.'

'What about after? Did they ever read the stories he wrote whilst he was over there?'

'They did read them and thought like the rest of the community that they were done in poor taste. My father threatened to burn them all one night after he returned from the club drunk. But he didn't.' I laugh.

Doctor Lin looks horrified that I have said this. I quickly add, 'He was just angry that Maugham had portrayed people like that. I have read them since and find that they are a fair description of what life was like back then; they aren't the worst stories I have heard about that time.'

'You have heard worse?'

'Well, yes, I'm afraid I have.'

I bite the top of my lip and look towards the back wall. I remember my mother did the same when she was thinking. What are you thinking about? I asked her as I climbed up on her knee. How I got so lucky having you, she would whisper into my ear. I shake my head and look down; my voice takes over before my mind can stop it.

'I remember one evening after my parents had been to the club with their friends, they all came back. Jimmy and I woke up and rushed into the front room thinking there would be another hoolie, you know. But everyone was sombre. Charlie Walsh started singing a very sad song. I asked my mother what was wrong and she said Geoffrey Gallagher had been killed that afternoon on his way into town. He had been shot. She had tears in her eyes. We have to be careful, Philip; these are dangerous times. Jimmy asked her why was he shot? She said it was because people were desperate. Times are hard. She said, I'm sure they didn't need to kill him they just got scared. I grabbed hold of her tightly. I remember I suddenly felt how vulnerable we were living there, that it was like what my father said, it wasn't our country. Of course, I couldn't translate that into words, but I knew we weren't safe, not completely.'

'Did they ever find the murderer?'

'No, they blamed the Chinese gangs. They were doing the rounds of the area robbing workers, selling counterfeit money. I guess if you fought back too hard they would shoot you. It was a bit like the old west. Strange times they were.'

I look towards my hands and suddenly hear my brother's voice. Come on, Philip, listen to me, we can figure this out. We just need to look for the clues, it's like Sherlock Holmes, we have to collect all the facts and make deductions. Come on! I clear my throat and look at Doctor Lin.

He nods and takes a sip of water. 'Did you and your brother play many games?'

'Yes.' I cough and reach for water. 'We played many games, made some up ourselves; although towards the end we didn't play that many, we had to help my father on his rounds. He made us check the trees, you know, that the rubber bowls were attached properly.'

'Didn't he have people for that?'

'Yes, yes he did but after Geoffrey Gallagher died my father stopped trusting a lot of people, he made us re-check things. Most of the time there was nothing wrong, sometimes there was. Once we found one of the tappers sitting underneath a tree. Jimmy and I walked over to him. I thought he was drunk, and I started to kick him, Jimmy started to shout at him, but he didn't move. I remember Jimmy squatting in front of him shouting for him to wake up, but he didn't. I knew then that something wasn't right; Jimmy told me to run and get our father. I ran as fast as I could, finding my father with a group of tappers by the south fence. I told him something happened. He jumped on the bike, and I sat behind him. We made it to Jimmy and the tapper. He is dead, Jimmy said as my father bent over and slapped the tappers face, he then checked his pulse. He stood back and nodded.'

'Do you know what he died of?'

'No, no idea. Probably one of those things you can never explain, you know like a weak heart or something. It went around though, local gossip that my father treated his workers so badly, that they were dying of starvation. The locals said it was because the fields were haunted and so the bomoh was called again to appease the angry spirits.' Doctor Lin looks at me surprised. 'I mean it happened not just in our plantation but in the others as well you know. People die sometimes, for weird and unexplained reasons, it's part of life. It's not like he hung himself from a tree or anything.'

'Did some of them do that?'

'Yes, quite a number of them. I remember in the neighbouring plantation one of their young workers hung himself in the middle of the night. There was also gossip around that, that he was in a relationship with another of the workers.'

'Oh, I see. You seem to know a lot about what was going on.'

I smile and rub my hands. 'Well, you know children, they pick up on everything and, well, we were bored. Jimmy said that we had to listen carefully to the adults, that they always gave themselves away if you listened carefully.' I rub my hand, it suddenly feels sore.

'I never liked being a child, you know, and I didn't like other children much even when I was a child. I was always pining to be an adult, to have more control and so I probably overheard too much but there was little else to do.'

He nods and grins at me, 'I understand completely.' I'm sure he does but he can't say anything about himself and that is what is weird about this. I can't ask him anything back, it isn't like a real conversation, one that I can control and bounce away from.

A door suddenly bangs. 'Someone is coming.' I whisper it but he hears me and looks up.

'What did you say, Mr Philip?'

'Someone is coming.'

'What do you mean?'

'Amah used to say that whenever the wind picked up and

banged the back door. It was a sign, someone is coming.'

'Did someone often come?'

'Yes, mostly men that worked with my father, not the tappers but other men, planters that helped him manage the plantation. I remember one man coming. He was young, fit, he had been working with my father for a month, fresh off the boat my father said. He came to speak to my father about his quarters, he was having trouble sleeping, he thought they were haunted.'

'Can you remember what he said?'

'Something about footsteps walking up and down the halls, about glass breaking but none of the windows were broken. He said someone grabbed him by his feet and wouldn't let him go. My father laughed, he told him to man up, that he was acting like a child but I remember this young man was afraid. He looked shaken and ashamed as my father spoke to him. He shook his head when my father suggested that perhaps he was just not used to the sounds of the jungle. No, Mr Goundry I am not, this is different. My father said there was no other space, it was either in that house or he had to live with the local workers. The young man, desperate, said he would rather live with the locals and so he did. A few weeks later there was a fire where some of the other quarters were destroyed and my father moved two other men into that house.'

'Did they complain about a ghost?'

'No,' I look out towards the roses that are swaying in the wind, 'no, they never did.' I swallow and stop myself from saying: but they suddenly left one night, took all their things and never returned.

'I remember waking up and hearing voices, strange sounds in the middle of the night, but we were on the edge of the jungle and I suppose it was normal to hear things like that. I remember one time I got up after hearing a cry. I went out to the veranda, it was like an animal was crying, but then it suddenly changed and it was like it was yelling. I must have been about six at the time and so I yelled out to it, stop, and then there was silence; a change in the jungle, then I heard Amah calling out my name, come inside, come inside, Philip, come inside now. There was something in her voice that sounded so serious and afraid, and I remember walking back inside. She grabbed my hands so tightly and said to me don't you ever answer those cries, do you hear me, there are evil spirits out there and all they want is to hurt you. You understand, don't you? I didn't understand of course, I didn't understand any of that, you don't as a child, you believe what you are told. My father would often say, children should be seen and not heard.' I laugh. Doctor Lin doesn't react, he suddenly looks sad.

I nod my head as if he has asked me something. 'But, yes, the Malays, they liked their superstitions. Do you believe in ghosts?' I ask him.

He stops the tape and grins at me, 'Yes, yes I do.'

'Seen one have you?'

'Yes, when I was a child, an old lady in the corner, she would sit in our kitchen, smiling, she had no teeth.'

'You weren't scared?'

'No, she wasn't evil, just sort of lonely. My parents hated it whenever I mentioned her; I stopped seeing her when we moved.'

'Did you ever see one again?'

'No, I never have. Have you?'

I nod and look down at my hands, 'Yes, I think so.'

'Was it when you were living on the plantation?'

'No, it was at school, and it wasn't a real ghost per se more like a presence, pretty bad one too.'

'Did you ever tell anyone about it?'

'Well, my school friends yes, but they already knew about it. Funny how old buildings are always considered haunted.'

'Some new buildings are also haunted. There is a new estate just built in the woodlands in Singapore that people have reported is haunted, built on an old shrine, I think.'

'Arousing old spirits.' I smile at him.

'Something like that.' He presses down the tape recorder again.

'So, with many people coming to the house did your father

have time to rest?'

'Oh yes, he did, normally he would go to bed around nine in the evening. My mother would stay up late on her own in the front room, she would normally read or sew.'

'I see. But they had visitors you said, hoolies?'

'Yes, dinners, entertaining, sometimes we had weeks when people came every day. On the weekends they went off to the club. Jimmy and I liked it when other people came to our house, we got to listen to news of what was going on in the other plantations, we got to hear what the gossip was.' I smile, 'I remember Jimmy started writing everything down, making notes of who came and what they said.'

'He did?'

'Yes, it was mainly for fun you know. He wrote down their conversations like they were characters in books. He was bored, I suppose, but he could always tell my parents who said what if they couldn't remember. Sometimes we would act out the conversations later; you know, make funny voices, hold up wine glasses and pretend we were drunk. I guess that is what got me started on being a writer.'

'How old were you then?'

'I was about eight or nine, Jimmy was thirteen.'

'Was there a lot of gossip?'

'Yes, but you see that's all we had, small diversions of news and gossip.' I laugh. 'I remember, there was a story of an

English woman gone mad who lived with her husband in the jungle. She would often wander around barely clothed with makeup smeared across her face talking to herself. There was gossip of other managers hitting their workers, not paying them and the workers would go to the bomoh and pay for them to put spells on their managers.'

'Did people believe in that?'

'Yes many did, some western women went to the bomoh to help them get pregnant or to help them to become, um, not pregnant.'

'Did you ever meet a bomoh?'

I nod. 'Once a year my father paid for our local one to come to the plantation and perform some sort of service. It was all very odd. I remember going close to him, but he pushed me away, after that I had to stay in the house every time he came. I don't know what I did to upset him, but he never wanted to see me again. I remember he came one time after Jimmy got bitten by a snake, a viper. We went with my father on one of his afternoon rounds and went off exploring in the jungle. I think Jimmy must have stepped on it. I remember him freezing, he looked terrified. I looked around thinking there was someone behind us but there wasn't. He didn't even cry out, he just stood so still, and I swear the blood drained out of his face. I rushed towards him and saw the snake slithering away under the fallen leaves, he bent over then and grabbed his ankle. I screamed and cried out for help and the tappers came running. My father arrived and scooped up my brother and we ran towards the car; the local workers went in search of the snake. Back then they wanted you to also catch the snake, so you knew for sure what it was that bit you. His leg swelled up and the veins that are normally hidden suddenly appeared, his leg was throbbing. It was quite a sight.'

'I can imagine.'

'Yes, yes it was, he didn't scream, tears fell down his face, he never said anything. I remember my mother wasn't at home and my father was angry.'

'Why did he become angry?'

'I don't know. Then she arrived back with a man; my father went outside and shouted at him.' Philip, she said, don't look outside, come on your brother needs you. I shake my head, 'I can't recall now.'

'Did you know the man?'

'No, no, I don't think so. I remember my father was furious, he came back in swearing. My mother ignored him. Hmm, funny what you remember. But then my brother's fever grew worse and he started to cough; he grew sick and my amah was convinced that they hadn't taken all of the poison out of him. She was worried that it would alter him.'

'Alter him?'

'Yes, he would become weak and demons would easily

enter his body and take over. Ular, snakes, help the demons travel. Anyway, he grew weaker and weaker and so they called the bomoh to come and I was banished for the day.'

'They took it very seriously that you could not see him.'

'I know, strange wasn't it?' I look away from his eyes, he knows it is bad if the bomoh doesn't want to see me; he knows that the bomoh knows something that others don't and if the bomoh doesn't like me it is because he thinks I am bad, evil.

'You never found out about the man who drove your mother?'

'No, well I never saw him, only his car parked outside. I just remember my father shouting and swearing.'

'What about later?'

'Nothing, it was never mentioned again. I often think we absorb more than we realise as children, our parent's moods, their laughter and tears, their screaming matches and their concerns.' I think to myself, that snake bite was the beginning of the end, perhaps a prophecy for what to was to come later.

'Did you ever return to the plantation in Kedah after you left?'

'You mean when I got older?'

'Yes,' he nods.

'No,' I shake my head. 'There was nothing to take me back. I am not the sort of person to reminisce.'

'But you returned to Singapore when you were older?'

I shift in my seat. 'Well, not right away. I worked for Imperial Oriental Shipping company for a few years in London. Then there was a war.' I cough. 'I served four years and luckily nothing too bad happened to me.'

'Where were you?'

'Oh, you know, everywhere. I don't really want to talk about it.' God knows I have written enough about it. 'After that I returned and moved back out to the East. I was lucky to get a new job with a shipping company. After the war, Singapore wasn't in great shape and they needed people, so I came back and worked at the ship terminal. I remember the day I arrived they were hanging six Japanese war criminals out in Changi. It was a pretty low-paid job, but I didn't care. I needed to get away from Europe after the war. They had to rebuild everything at the port, the Japanese had done a real job destroying much of Singapore's infrastructure. It was like rebuilding a city from scratch. It was quite a dangerous city back then; people were angry, there was a lot of unrest, little food, no electricity, people were desperate. We'd often have small crowds of people standing outside the entrance of the port begging for food. The city was overcrowded, there wasn't enough housing. Chinatown was packed, people living in squalid conditions, mortality rates were higher than they were during the war. You know we used Japanese prisoners of war to help rebuild the port; it was part of their penance, working fourteen-hour days. They had one day off, well the government said they did but I don't think they did. I stayed out of their way. I was hired by R.S. Tyrone Shipping. They weren't as big as they are today, they were just setting up out there and I was hired to go and set it up. Initially the harbour authorities did not want us but after a large amount of money exchanged hands we had permission. We were the first ones that started to sort out the backlog; the port was chaotic, disorganised and we started to help implement changes. The black market is what kept the city alive back then, it was what paid for the electricity, gas and water to be fixed as quickly as it was.'

He nods.

'Anyway, I didn't stay long, only a couple of months.'

'Why didn't you stay?'

'I met my wife and we decided to move back to Europe.'

'Your wife was living in Singapore?'

'Yes, she had grown up there, her father had worked in the customs office. She had been sent with her mother and sister to Perth during the war and she had just returned. She was planning on going back to Europe.'

'So how long did you stay?'

'Eight months.'

Tom knocks and Doctor Lin stops the tape.

'Sorry, it is time for his check-up.'

'Of course.' Doctor Lin gets up and starts to pack his stuff away.

I say, 'Oh, you can stay if you want to, it won't take long.'

Doctor Lin looks at me. 'No, it is okay, we are done for today. I don't want to tire you out.'

'If you say so. I am not tired.' Tom looks at me surprised. 'I'm not,' I say, defiant. I suppose I sound like a child again not wanting to go back to bed but the truth is I am not tired, I feel great. It's been so long since I have talked about this and I could keep on going. I had forgotten so much but it's all starting to unravel, fall back into place. I don't want to lose momentum.

Doctor Lin smiles. 'Well, I will come back after lunch.'

'No,' I say as Tom rolls up my sleeve to check my blood pressure.

'No, you can stay. Right, Tom? We have enough for Doctor Lin, don't we?'

'Of course we do.'

'Then stay, please,' I say. 'I am alright, aren't I Tom?'

'You are right as rain, Philip. Sit yourself down, Doctor Lin, and I'll grab your lunches.'

Doctor Lin grins gratefully.

I say, 'The food here is excellent.'

'I know, I remember from last time. You are very lucky, Mr Philip.'

'Yes I am,' I reply proudly.

'You have many more people to interview?'

'No, you are my only one.'

'Am I?'

'Yes, I am doing lots of research in the archives, so I only have time for one.'

'I see.'

'Research mostly about the rubber plantations in Malaya, yours and the other plantations surrounding yours.'

'Ah, I see.' Tom wheels in a tray table with our plates. He sets it up for us and I tell Doctor Lin that Tom is always so good to me, I think he likes me best.

Tom laughs, 'I'm only doing this because I'm hoping you're going to remember me in your estate.' We all laugh, Tom is kind and gentle with me, more than anyone else has been in years.

Today we eat gammon for lunch, a slice of tinned pineapple with two small, boiled potatoes and a small salad that consists of a lettuce leaf and two quarters of a tomato. The meal looks depressingly small served on a large round white plate. I want to tell him that there will be seconds but there never is and I don't want to lie.

'Ginger cake for afters,' Tom said when he wheeled in the food.

Doctor Lin eats slowly. He bends his head down and he takes bites; he must think this food is so bland he is probably used to eating spicy noodles in chicken broth, or barbecue duck with fluffy white rice.

'The food we ate when I was growing up wasn't very good. Of course, I didn't realise that until I went to school in England. Can you imagine boarding school food being better than that you were served at home?' He looks at me and then looks at the tape recorder. 'Oh of course, I apologise, we should wait until we start again, I guess that is also of interest?'

He nods enthusiastically, 'Yes it is, if you could wait please.'

I nod, chewing on the gammon. It is rubbery, almost undercooked. I would have spat it out if he wasn't sitting opposite me.

'What did your father do?' I suddenly ask him.

'Oh.' He stops eating and immediately pats down his mouth with a tissue he has taken from his pocket. 'He was a schoolteacher.'

'Oh yes?'

'Yes, he taught high school children in Singapore.'

'I see. What did he teach?'

'Maths.'

'Was he well liked?'

'Yes,' he nods, 'I think so.' I notice he doesn't touch the pineapple but only stares at it. I presume he will leave it till the end thinking it is a dessert. 'He was a very strict man,' he adds.

'He was?'

71

'Yes, very strict, studying always came before anything else. On weekdays I wasn't allowed to play with my friends or play games outside. I had to study.'

'That must have been hard.'

He nods. 'He wanted me to be a doctor.'

'Well, you are a doctor.'

'No, a medical doctor. He wasn't happy that I ended up working for the archives, researching and teaching.'

'He probably was thrilled but did not know how to show it.'

'No, he said I wasted my life. Threw away all my hard work looking at the past and studying things that didn't matter when I should have been saving people's lives, I should have contributed to society. He was a great admirer of Lee Kuan Yew. He campaigned and worked with him at the beginning of the new Singapore. He was so proud of it, so proud we have moved on. He would have hated that I am looking back now to that past, he would say it was beneath me.' He sighs and looks mournfully at the pineapple.

'Do you not like pineapple?'

'I do but it's warm, I'm waiting until it cools.' He looks at his watch.

'Is your father dead?'

He nods. 'Yes, he died five years ago.'

'I'm sorry.'

He shrugs his shoulders, 'I didn't see him often, maybe twice a year, he was living with my sister and her family.'

'Did you not get along with them?'

'No, I do. I am just very busy with work, there are only two of us working at the moment on the oral transcripts.'

'I see. And your research?'

'Well, that is just mine, so I have to work on that with no help.'

'What are you planning to do with all the research you have uncovered?'

'Write a book about it, there aren't many books written about that time.'

'I can't understand why not. My father did not treat his workers badly and he paid them, I can imagine some of the other plantation owners were not as kind?'

'No, they weren't.' He doesn't add anything to this, and I put down my fork. I suddenly feel that he blames me and my family for all the wrongdoing of that time.

'You know my parents went out there for a better life, like many of the Tamils and the Chinese, they wanted to have better opportunities.'

He scrunches up his forehead. He says, 'But Mr Philip, the workers, the tappers, never made that much money even when there was a boom, most of the money always went to the Europeans, to the British Government.'

'Yes, but ...'

'And the Tamils were taken away from their families. They had to save up for years to be able to afford to go home, and look at Malaysians today. There are still some people tapping rubber in the same way for little or no money. All of this comes from an industry created to fund the British Empire, leaving little for the locals. They don't have much of a choice, it's either tap trees or starve. I think it was, and is, very different for them than it was for you.'

'I know, I didn't mean anything, only that my father wasn't that bad.'

'No one ever wants to think that their father is bad,' he says looking away from me.

Tom enters with a huge grin on his face, carrying a tray. 'So, I managed to get you both the biggest pieces of ginger cake and made you a pot of tea.' He places it down. 'I also got you some custard, mind you that ginger cake is wet enough if you ask me.'

Doctor Lin says thank you and I smile.

'I'll clear those plates for you.'

We sit in silence and it's awkward. I want to say things, important intelligent things about how much they did, how they helped, how they established bridges, infrastructure, but I can't find the words. I sit muted, my tongue going over my teeth, something I have started to do when I want to speak but can't find the words; my tongue still gets its exercise.

Doctor Lin removes the pineapple with his fingers as Tom lifts the plates. He lets it slide down his finger, there is no juice, it is dry, he places it on top of one of the bowls with custard and he grabs it greedily and starts to eat before my plate is cleared.

Tom laughs, 'I hope you enjoyed that.' He gives me a wink and walks out with the tray and our dirty plates. I watch him eat and feel sick. I push away the ginger cake and stare out towards the hallway, trying to avoid the sounds he is making,

Wednesday Afternoon

'Why did you leave R.S. Tyrone Shipping?'

'Bored, to be honest. They tried to keep me but I met my wife and then we returned back to her home. We moved back to Buckinghamshire to her family's old house, then we had our son and, well, my wife unfortunately passed away. Her parents then moved back and lived close by; they were very good to me, very supportive of my career, they practically adopted me as their own son.'

'What about her sister?'

'She also died young, killed by a speeding car on River Valley Road. Tragic really.'

I stare down confused. 'How death seems to follow me.' I say this aloud and he looks at me, his eyes opened wide, surprised.

'No, no, Mr Philip, not everyone can keep up.' I smile at him thankful that he is trying to make me feel better.

'I suppose not. I didn't ever think I would live this long. But I guess it is good for you I did, at least you have me as a source.'

'Well, you are a great source, Mr Philip, like your books

about the Second World War, they are wonderful.'

'Thank you,' I say. Books I can't stand the sight of now.

'Did you never want to write about your childhood?'

'No, I never wanted to write anything about it. I suppose it always seemed as if I would but no I didn't. I didn't think it would sell.'

'Oh, I think it would.'

'Yes, well it is too late for that now.'

The books, the stories, none of it real, none of it important despite what they say. All those stories I stole from young men that died, that I retold for my own monetary gain. I was nothing but a charlatan. That's the thing about age, nothing seems that important, only living.

'The last time you were in Singapore you stayed at Raffles?'

'Yes, I did. It was lovely but it had changed. Singapore had changed a lot. It was different but still the same in a way. There were no rickshaws, instead you have the nicest, most educated taxi drivers in the world. Some of them had read me and wanted to discuss my books. They said that I should write about Singapore, said that I should tell the world what was happening under the surface.' He stops then and looks at me as if I have sworn. He stops the tape. I say, 'I should know better by now, I am sorry. I didn't mean to offend you.'

'No, please, don't worry, it isn't you. I will delete that though before it goes through the archives.'

I say quickly, 'Of course, I understand. I love Singapore. It was where I was born. Despite all I have been through it is still my home.' I say this fast. I'm lying, it never felt like home.

Thursday

Today, I haven't been very honest or open to him. I keep repeating myself: 'I can't recall', 'I don't know', 'maybe it will come back to me' or 'please, I need a break', 'please pass me my water', 'please, we need to stop'. Sometimes my memory is sharp, as sharp as the needles Tom sinks into my old skin. Drugs to help me relax, drift off, lie in the creek that I used to as a boy and stare up as the clouds float above me; they were always moving, always on their journey to more important places, like Europe and America. We weren't important living out there then.

He smells of garlic. I lift my arm and reach for my water that is still standing from yesterday, untouched. Yesterday was a good day, I slept fourteen hours. His teeth aren't good, they are crooked, he needs to go to a dentist. He should have gone as a child, he doesn't come from money then, despite his glasses and shoes. He had entered excited; it had been some time since I had last seen him. In between that time, I have started to relearn Latin, no time like the present, it helps train the brain. I always liked languages I think I just never took the time to really learn them and keep them up.

Femina domi dormit sed Vir non domi dormit.

It reminds me of Italian and French. I start to think back to the Romans. They built roads, established routes, they gave us so much, all roads lead to Rome. I doubt there is a road that leads from Rome to Cullodena, but I could be wrong.

'Are you ready to start again?'

I nod, 'I haven't seen you for a while.'

'No, Mr Philip, I was here.'

I shake my head. That is impossible. I am about to say no, that was weeks ago but he interrupts me. He speaks fast. 'So, Mr Philip, I did manage to find something on the abandoned house in your plantation,' he says. He places down some papers right in front of me. 'I went to the archives,' he proudly announces. 'I found some things on the death of a woman.'

'Oh,' I say, moving in my seat, 'there was a woman after all? Hopefully not a demon though.' I suddenly remember a young girl's face; she hisses at me.

'Yes.' He nods enthusiastically, he is happy. I suppose for him it is like unlocking a hidden secret. I hear my mother's voice. No more secrets, Philip, I promise. Someone is coming, get ready.

'I thought Amah was lying.'

'No,' he shakes his head, 'not at all. A western woman by the name of Helen James was found dead, hanging at the front door.'

'Oh …' I speak. He shows me a copy of an article, *Straits Times*, 1910. He has enlarged it. 'That was before we moved there.'

'Yes, I know.'

'Do they know why?'

'No, only that she had taken her life. She was married to Gavin James. He was the former plantation owner before your father.'

'Oh, I see.'

'The plantation was left vacant for about two years after that. Did you know that no one ran it?'

'No, I didn't.'

'Your father had his work cut out for him; it must have been in a bad state.'

I nod.

'Do you know why she killed herself?' He asks me this as if he knows the answer. I am suddenly afraid.

'No, I don't. I was just a child.'

'You remember meeting Gavin James?'

'No, I don't.'

'Your father never mentioned him?'

'No, and I already told you about the house.'

'Yes, you did. Although I did also find out that a similar thing happened after you left for school?'

'What?' I sit up now. 'What do you mean a similar thing?'

'There was a young woman found dead in that abandoned house.'

'What? What woman?'

'Well, it's says an unidentified young local woman, her body was found, she had been shot. No one was ever charged with her murder.'

'What? Let me see that.' I snatch it off him, 1930. 'My father died that year.'

'Yes,' he coughs, 'he died a month before. Of fever, yes?'

'Yes. Well, that's what I was told.'

'The plantation was then sold on, wasn't it?'

'Yes, yes it was.'

'Do you ever remember seeing a local woman around the house?'

'I told you already, we had staff, there were plenty of them.'

'Yes, yes of course, but what about by the abandoned house, do you ever remember seeing anyone there?'

I snap at him, 'No, I told you we weren't allowed to go there'. I close my eyes tight, I don't want to see her again, Jimmy said she was a *pontianak*. Pontianak, vampire girl. She hissed like a snake.

'Yes, of course, so sorry.' He looks down, his expression so pathetic.

I'm angry, I don't know what he is trying to say but I don't like it. 'I don't know what you want me to say.'

'Nothing, only what you remember. I just thought some of this would help to trigger some memories.'

'Well, it doesn't. If you ask me, you are just trying to put into my head events that just didn't happen and things that weren't even there.'

'So sorry.'

'Why do you need to find out about all of this, what has it to do with history anyway?'

He looks away from me and switches off the tape recorder. We sit in silence. I stare at him, waiting for an apology, but he doesn't say anything. I sigh. I suppose I should talk about it, perhaps it will make sense. I start to speak.

'Fine. Amah said there was a pontianak living in the abandoned house, a ghost vampire woman looking to trap men. The demon that lived in that house.'

He holds up his hand and I stop speaking. 'Please wait, Mr Philip.' I wait and he nods. From the beginning please. He turns the tape recorder back on.

I sigh. 'Amah said there was a pontianak living in the abandoned house. A pontianak is a ghost vampire that is looking to trap men. She said the only way to make sure it was a ghost was to bend over and look at her feet; ghosts don't walk on land you see. Every society has its myths. I remember hearing the cries of some animal one night and Amah would say that is the pontianak, but she is far away; the louder her cries the further she is away, the quieter her cries the closer she is. I never heard her come nearby but Amah told me never to go to the house, they said that she was hiding in there and all she would do is kill and eat me and my brother. One day Jimmy and I came upon a trail of leaves leading up to the abandoned house. The leaves were folded in a special way, you know, like origami.' I'm using my hands to try and tell him how they looked; by his facial expression I am not doing a good job. 'I remember I collected them in my pockets and then buried them in our garden.'

'Why would you bury them?'

'I don't know. I don't remember. I was scared. Amah said that pontianak lived in the trees, banana trees she said, they were dangerous and so I thought I would bury them. You know make them disappear.'

He looks at me as if I have said something wrong. 'I was a child. I didn't know any better.'

'Did you see these origami leaves often?'

I shake my head. I am about to say no, but something stops me. 'There was another time.'

'Did you bury them too?'

'No.' I shake my head. But Doctor Lin isn't looking at me, he is looking at his watch. I stop talking and let the silence take over, we sit and he is staring off into space and for a moment I believe he has eyes like a cat, like a tiger. I shift in my seat, something has changed, something bad. I cough and ask, 'Are we nearly finished?'

'Oh,' Doctor Lin jolts and turns his eyes to me, 'are you tired, Mr Philip?'

'No, I just thought I was boring you.' I give him a timid smile. I want him to go. Something is wrong, I can feel it.

'No, you aren't, not at all, all of this is so valuable.' I don't believe him when he says it. How could me remembering about Amah and her strange ways be valuable to anyone?

He reaches into his bag and takes out a folder. 'Have you ever heard of the myth of the Red Pied Piper?'

'The fairy tale?'

'No.' He clears his throat and leans forward. He speaks softly.

'The Red Pied Piper, it was a ... how do you say ... an urban legend that came out of that time. Many people still talk about the Red Pied Piper in Malaysia today, the man with the children, he would apparently travel throughout the jungle with a group of children, and he would kill people.'

I immediately look away from him. He continues talking. 'He was a demon; I believe the children were those that he had killed, and they travelled with him. He was like a warning to small children, to not go too deep into the jungle or the Red Pied Piper would come and get you.'

I shake my head. 'I never heard that.'

'No?'

'No, never. I suppose every area has its own myths and legends; we had the pontianak.'

'I just wondered whether The Red Pied Piper myth had anything to do with the killing of some of the plantation managers.'

'I don't believe so. I would have heard about him. It was as far as I could remember the Chinese gangs.'

'I see.'

'I mean, occasionally we did have people that travelled through selling things and transporting children from the orphanages to work in the plantations further north.' I cross my forehead, I see his bracelets, his tanned arms. 'I suppose …' I start, do I really want to go down this hole? I don't look at Doctor Lin, I feel his eyes though, I feel them waiting. 'I suppose,' I start again, my voice takes over and my mind is numb, 'there was someone that could have been called the Red Pied Piper, he definitely had a red beard and he transported young girls further north, but he was harmless.'

'Can you remember his name?'

'No, I'm sorry I can't.' I can, but I haven't said it for years.

'Did he come to your house?'

'No.' I look towards the floor pretending to search my mind. The flute. My father shouting, Come on Red play us another one.

I say, 'I can't remember. I don't think so. It is all so long ago. I can't recall. That's a strange myth though. The Red Pied Piper, like the German myth.'

'Very similar. People would say, "*Berhati-hati dengan Mat Salleh berjanggut merah*." Be careful of the red-bearded white man.'

'It is an odd myth.' I shake my head.

'One that is still there today.'

'Is that right?' His laugh, his beard rust red, his cap. He said to me as I stroked the marking on his hand, those witches lad, are after me, but they will never get me.

I shudder and Doctor Lin sits up, 'Are you alright?'

'Yes, fine, someone just walked over my grave.' Doctor Lin looks shocked. 'You know the expression, don't you?'

'Yes, I have heard it.'

'I seem to get them a bit more than I used to, must be my old nervous system.'

He stares at me. He knows I'm trying to hide something. I can feel it. 'Are we done for now?'

'Yes,' he nods, 'yes we are.'

'Good.' I reach and pull down the rope.

He nods, stands up and delivers me a small bow, takes his things and leaves. The room is bright, the sun beaming, time for longer days and warmer nights. I shiver, I am suddenly cold, and I close my eyes wishing I felt the humidity of the jungle. I wish I was warm throughout my body; back to those sticky nights, a storm rumbling in the distance, lightning and thunder and then torrential showers of rain muting the noises of the house, the jungle and the singing. Pale orchids in the morning that had been swept into our garden by soft winds. My mother placing one behind her ear, she dances for us, and we giggle as my father ignores her as he stares out towards the road. Someone is coming, he says. Someone is coming, someone he does not know.

Friday Morning

'It was an unusual way to grow up, Mr Philip. It must have been a strange and wonderful time.'

'It wasn't wonderful,' I sigh, 'it was hard and miserable. Nothing was ever what it seemed.' I have had enough now – memories, strange images, odd thoughts that invade my mind like a swarm of flies. I now think it is naive to ever think a time was once idyllic or that I was ever lucky, someone was always paying a price for my happiness.

I look down at my old hands. I rub them. Whatever happened to the plump smooth hands I used to have, why is skin so weak, why does it lose its elasticity and dry up and erode, why can't it just be like a tree and renew itself.

'What do you mean nothing was as it seemed, Mr Philip?'

'The jungle isn't a place for man, Doctor Lin. It's like what we did to those trees, the jungle chisels away at you until you are left standing torn and bare, oozing blood and sweat. It takes away everything you know and makes you into someone else, someone you never knew you could become. Someone that isn't good per say, nor evil, but someone that lies beneath us all, someone more primitive.'

'Primitive?'

'Yes. Civilised man does not belong in the jungle, he can stay for a few years but beyond that he will not last. It's the heat you see, the isolation, the sounds, the animals, it does something to you. Makes you become aware of other parts of yourself, removes you from the obligations of society. Eventually you just become a man in the jungle, a human, just another animal competing for survival.' He doesn't answer me but looks down at the copies of the newspaper articles he has made. I suddenly say, 'The leaves.'

'Leaves?' He looks up and pushes his glasses further into his face.

'Leaves, trails of them that led to the abandoned house.'

'You mentioned that yesterday.'

'Was it only yesterday?' Time has little meaning for me anymore.

'I saw them more than twice. I saw them daily. We used to follow them like it was a game but then we stopped.'

'Why did you stop?'

'We saw something.'

'What did you see?'

'Something no child should ever see.'

'Was it the woman?'

'I don't know if it was her, but there was a girl and a man.'

'Oh.' He looks away embarrassed.

I look down. I say, 'It isn't what you think. They weren't copulating.'

'They weren't?'

'No.' I shake my head and take a deep breath in. Here we go. 'She was helping him put on stockings.'

'Oh, you mean he was helping her put on stockings.'

'No, I don't, I mean she was helping him, he was wearing a dress, a green dress.'

He looks at me confused. 'Did you know this man?

I nod, I don't want him to ask me, he seems to feel that and he doesn't. But he stops the tape and stares at me.

'My father was an odd man you see, the jungle made him odder I believe, it made him more dangerous to himself and to us.'

'I see, Mr Philip, I am sorry. I didn't realise.'

'It wasn't very common you see.'

'No, I know.'

'It still isn't, I think.' I wipe away tears.

'Did you tell anyone?'

'No, no one. I tried to talk about it to Jimmy, but he told me to be quiet, that it wasn't our father, it was the demon, he had taken to looking like him. I said how can we be sure that he doesn't come into our house if he looks like our father? He said we'd know because the demon likes to wear women's clothes and our father wouldn't wear them so it's only when we see our father in women's clothes then we will know. I believed Jimmy and tried to forget about it.'

'He never saw you, your father?'

'No, well, I don't think he did, he never mentioned it and he treated us the same.'

'And the girl? The leaves?' He turns on the tape recorder again.

'Sometimes I could hear singing but in the jungle you always heard voices without anyone being there. But we did see her one day, she stood in front of us grinning. No teeth. Her clothes dirty, ripped. I immediately turned around and bent over and looked through my legs to see if she was a ghost. She isn't one of them, I said to my brother.'

'One of what?'

'Pontianak.'

'Do you really believe she was one?'

'When you're a child you believe that those things exist. We were told by Amah that the gods wear human forms, so we had to be careful. Demons were common back then, there was always some story going around about someone seeing some demon or vampire.'

He smiles at me. 'Sometimes when you're not a child you also believe. What did she want?'

'I can't remember. Oh, I think Jimmy shouted at her, told her to get away, that she was on private property, that he would call our father. The girl didn't react, she was strange, she just stood there grinning. I remember Jimmy spoke to her in Malay, told her to get away. *Pergi! Pergi!* But she didn't do anything. He threw rocks at her; she just stood there. It was very eerie.' I shudder. 'The jungle went so quiet. I then remember a great huge python slithered out onto the road, drawing a line between us. We stood back and she hissed at us, the girl not the snake, and then ran off back to the abandoned house. We ran home. We didn't tell anyone about it.'

'You didn't?'

'No, you see the police were already there when we returned, there had been another killing of a plantation manager. The third one that year.'

'What?' He stares at me shocked. 'Three managers dead?'

'Yes, all shot. By the end of that year I think six had been killed.'

'What?'

'Yes. Shot dead, some in their houses, some in the fields and some biking home.' I speak without looking at him. 'All of them had been robbed – money, watches, rings taken. Some of them were my parents' friends, the ones they had over after club.'

'That is a lot of plantation managers to lose in one year.'

'I know. I remember my father mentioning it was the Chinese gangs.'

Doctor Lin looks down confused.

'It sounds strange, doesn't it.' Jimmy's voice sounds in my head. Philip, you promise, we can't tell anyone, it's too dangerous.

'Yes, it does. Can I show you a photograph I found in the archives? I was wondering whether you could let me know if you knew these men?'

He hands it over to me and I see them, both of them. I start to shake. 'My father,' I say. I remember him finding me. You have no business following me, none at all. Stop it, Philip, stop crying. I'll give you something to cry about. His belt, heavy thick tears seeping into the jungle ground. You're too weak, he said as he struck me, like your mother. I can't stop shaking and Doctor Lin looks at me concerned, tape recorder off and he pulls down on the rope.

'Michelle? Tom?' he calls out. 'Something is happening. Help!'

Someone is coming, she whispers to me, my mother, get ready, Philip, someone is coming.

Monday Morning

He smiles. 'Mr Philip, can we talk about the photograph that I showed you. The one with your father and that man next to him.'

I look at him surprised. He isn't messing about now, he knows something, or he saw something behind my eyes when he showed me the photograph. My father standing on the veranda with him, both grinning, shotguns to the side of them. I shut down but he must have seen something.

'The photograph?' I reply slowly. I'm not going to give much away. I'll play the old man card. I clear my throat, 'I can't recall.'

'Yes, the photograph with your father.'

He passes it to me again. I pretend. 'How did you know it was my father?'

'You said, my father.'

I look at it, my eyes stare into my father's. He is young, fit and happy. I look behind him to the right and see the cane chairs that my mother sat in. Maybe I don't need to pretend, it isn't hurting anyone me talking like this, they are all dead. Their voices are only weightless ghosts that reside in me. I'm sure I can control them. I don't need to be afraid anymore.

'I remember.' I relax into my voice, as if I am an actor retelling a story already written. 'I remember playing in the house and walking out onto the veranda. My father and mother were sitting on those rattan chairs, my mother was crying, my father was holding her hands. I don't know why she was crying, but they looked so serious, especially to a young boy. I left them, almost afraid of what was being said.'

'How old were you then?'

'I don't know, around eight.'

'Do you know what they were discussing?'

'No, but I remember it was the first time I had ever seen my mother crying. She was tough, she looked as if she would be more at home on a farm in Scotland than managing the bungalow of a plantation.' My thumb gently rubs the side of the photograph, I don't look at the other man.

'What about that man next to your father, do you remember him?'

'No.' I put down the photograph.

'Please look at the photograph, Mr Philip.' His tone suddenly alters, his voice stern like my old master at school.

I look down at the picture. I see him, his beard, his shirt, Angus Sinclair. The strange bracelets he wore. 'He once told me as I played with a bracelet that it was made for me by a witch, to ward off all those crazy Chinese witches. I can never take it off, he said to me, or else I would be dead.

You would die?

Yes, all their spells would get to me. This bracelet is my secret power, it makes sure no spells get through.

What kind of spells?

Spells that would make me sick, cause me to have an accident, spells that would cause me to die. Those witches they cut off your hair, take a piece of your clothes and then they go and see another witch and they make spells.

I stopped playing with it and backed away.

I remembered he laughed, don't worry, don't worry, kid, nothing will happen. This bracelet will never fall off.'

I sit back and smile and Doctor Lin looks at me. He speaks. 'Can you remember what kind of bracelet it was?'

'What?'

'The bracelet, did it have any markings or signs on it?'

'You heard me talking about the bracelet?'

'Yes, and the Chinese witches.'

'Oh.' I sit back, my mind, my mind it is giving me away. I can't control it. Be careful, Philip. I sit for a while and keep my lips closed shut, how much else has he heard, what else does he know. 'Hmm,' I eventually sound and swallow.

'The bracelet?'

'It was woven, dark red, it had a funny symbol, carved on a small shell or a piece of ivory. I have never seen one like it again.'

'How often did he come to your house?'

I shrug my shoulders. 'Careful.' I whisper but he has heard me.

'Mr Philip?'

'Once, maybe twice a month.'

'He did business with your father?'

'Yes, I suppose so. I can't really recall what he did.'

'Do you remember I mentioned something about the Red Pied Piper.'

I gasp. Jimmy's voice, Philip, you promise you can't tell anyone. 'No, no, I don't want to talk about him.'

'Why don't you want to talk about him?'

'I don't, it's not right, we shouldn't be talking about such things. I told you everything I knew.'

'Was this man bad?' He points to Angus, next to my father. They are grinning, they are happy.

I nod. 'Amah used to call him the devil, she used to sing old songs in Chinese when he entered the house. Loud old songs about banishing the devil, about getting rid of him.'

'Do you think he was the Red Pied Piper?'

I shake my head, 'I don't know. I don't … but I just feel that we shouldn't talk about him.'

'This man is dead; he can't get you.'

I shake my head. I feel myself wanting to cry. This is silly, an old man like me crying about him.

Doctor Lin sighs and continues, 'You knew him well?'

'Sort of.'

'He was kind to you?'

'Monsters are always kind to me, Doctor Lin. I don't know why but they always seem to like me.'

'What do you mean by monsters?'

'Men like him, bad men, evil men, men that should have been drowned at birth.'

'Why do they always like you?'

'I don't know. Amah said it was because I was born under an auspicious moon. She said gods would protect me. I used to think she was lying but over the years I have come to think there was truth in what she was saying.'

'That you are protected from evil men?'

I nod. 'It sounds crazy, I know.' I start to shiver.

'Maybe we should take a break, Mr Philip.' He goes to stop the tape recorder.

'No, I say, no. You want to know about him then I will tell you, but I doubt you will ever want it to be known. You'll never want him to be part of your history.'

'But he is part of our history no matter what he did. We need to know. Please tell me about him.'

'His name was Angus Sinclair; he had a red beard. My father called him Red. He transported orphan girls throughout the Straits to work at the outlaying plantations. He would collect the girls from the convents in Singapore and deliver them to various plantations and houses so they could work as domestic helpers.'

'He doesn't sound like the devil.'

'No, I know.' I nod. I look away, I don't want to think of him.

'How old were the girls that he transported?'

'All ages. I can't remember.'

'Did you ever meet any of them?

'No. When he would come to our house on the way through the Straits they would sit in his wagon and wait. I used to look out at them from my window. They would sit under the old mango tree outside. Amah would bring them water and treats. I remember Jimmy one time opened the window and threw rocks at them; one time I threw down a thin black snake, it landed close to them, and they started screaming.'

'Did Angus Sinclair ever harm the girls?'

'No,' I laugh nervously. 'No, he wasn't like that.'

'I mean ...'

'I know what you mean. No, he didn't. He didn't like young girls.'

'How do you know for sure?'

'I don't, I just think he didn't.' That is the truth I didn't know. I didn't know for sure. His hand on that knee could have meant something else. 'He never seemed to pay them any attention. He would allow Amah to give them water and feed them, but I never saw him look upon them and when he was transporting them he never drank. It was the times he wasn't working that were the problem.'

'The problem?'

'Yes, he drank too much and, well, he made my father drink too much. He was a bad influence on him.'

'Did your mother like him?'

'I don't know. I think she put up with him for my father's sake. He always brought presents, you know whisky, canned fruit and fabric for my mother. I remember my parents laughed a lot when he was around. He was a strange man but funny and his accent was so strong sometimes I couldn't understand what they were talking about. But it was the drink that changed him, he would drag my father out into the jungle to do things.' Philip, get away from the window!

'What kind of things?'

'I can't recall.' Philip, stop! Go to your brother. Someone is coming.

'You can't recall?'

'Not exactly. Sometimes they would go out into the jungle, and we would hear gunshots and laughter. They liked to shoot in the dark at small animals. Like it was a drunken game.'

'What about your mother?'

I look away. 'I don't know if I should say this. I don't want to, it was so long ago.'

'If it was so long ago then you should say it.'

'My mother had had enough one evening. They had woken me and my brother and we were crying – it was scary to be in the jungle and to hear the sounds of gunshots and laughter. The jungle was normally loud but whenever they entered it, everything went quiet; it's like the trees and the animals were watching them. My mother heard a gunshot and ran out furious.'

'What happened then?'

I don't speak. I hold my breath. I have kept this part a secret for so long, I hardly know whether it is true or not. I remember her hands; how petite they were and the lines of her veins that had started to poke out. I would trace them as I cried, and she would hold me close. 'Sometimes she would sing to us, sometimes she would give us warm condensed milk to help us sleep. I would fall into such a deep sleep I could hardly remember where I was when I awoke, I almost believe I was drugged.'

'You do?'

I cough. 'What did I say?' My mind is giving me away again. Slow down, control, control. Be careful, Philip.

'You said that you thought the milk your mother gave you was drugged.'

'Oh,' I start to shake a little. 'I'm not sure, but my brother said he thought she did.'

'What happened when your mother went out that night?'

'I don't know.' I bite down on my lip. Someone is coming, get ready Philip.

'We started to drift off to sleep, I remember seeing the back of her dress, burnt orange, when she left our room and that was it. We never saw her again.' I wipe a tear away. 'They said she had left, had enough, packed her bags, taken her clothes and gone in the night, that she had a lover and he had taken her back to Singapore.'

'Did you think that was true?'

Philip, get ready.

'No, no I don't.' I pause and bite down harder on my lower lip, it was all so long ago. I look up at him. 'You see, all her clothes had gone missing and the cane suitcase my parents used sometimes when they went to Singapore had gone. My father convinced everyone that she had gone, that she had taken a lover and left him and us. Amah didn't believe it. I don't know about the workers and the servants.'

'Did you believe it?'

'No, I didn't. About a week later my brother and I were playing outside and my brother threw a stick and I went to get it. I went into the jungle very loudly, you know you have to in case of tigers, anyway that's when I saw it, her suitcase. I opened it and saw that all her clothes and shoes were inside.'

'Did you tell your father?'

'No, I didn't. I never told anyone, not even Jimmy.'

He looks at me curiously, his arm reaches up and stops the tape. I blink at him, he sighs.

'What is wrong?' I ask.

He bends forward and clasps his hands together. He takes off his glasses, they leave indented imprints on his face. I think he must have been wearing the same pair of glasses for years, I wonder whether he sleeps in them? You can't sleep in glasses though, that is crazy but maybe these are sleeping glasses; maybe that is what people do now, wear glasses in bed. His feet shift and for a moment I think I see something, fur, an animal or a tail.

He speaks. 'Your mother went missing, you found her suitcase and you didn't think to ever say anything to anyone about it?'

'No, I didn't, well I couldn't, who was I going to tell, and they wouldn't listen to me. I was a child, and my father, well, I wasn't ready to go against him, he changed after she left.'

Doctor Lin sighs, 'I just have a hard time believing this.'

I shrug. 'Well, that's what happened.'

'Are you lying?'

'Why would I lie?'

'I don't know.'

'I am only telling you what I remember, that is what you wanted, wasn't it? That is why you came all this way to see me, that is why you brought the photograph, isn't it?'

He looks up at me and puts his glasses on again, he glances at the photograph.

'The photograph, so why did you bring the photograph? Why did you want me to talk about Angus Sinclair? You already knew about him, didn't you?'

He shakes his head. 'No, no, but ...' and he starts to whisper. It's soft, I can't hear it.

'I can't hear you, speak up, I'm ninety-three after all.' I laugh to try and lighten the mood. I do this for people to feel better about me saying how old I am. Ninety-three, that is ancient, my great granddaughter says, you are ancient like the pharaohs on the Nile.

'I found something,' he says. I don't say anything but swallow. I'm suddenly afraid. Someone is coming, Philip, you better get ready. 'I found some records in the archives, a list found in the contents of a former police station in Kedah.'

'A list?'

'Yes,' he looks at the tape, 'a list of men. It lists their ages, whether they were married and where they worked.'

'Uh huh.' I feel I know where he is going with this. Philip, get out! Don't look at it, it isn't finished. I said get out!

'A list of men's names that all had the same job.'

105

'Yes?'

'Yes, they were all plantation managers.'

'Oh, I see.'

'You know what the most interesting thing about this list is?'

I don't reply, I don't need to.

'Each of these men was murdered.'

'Oh,' I reply.

'And on the bottom of the list is his name, Angus Sinclair. It is circled. So, Mr Philip, do you recall the death of Charlie Walsh who died in 1919 from an apparent suicide, a gunshot to the head?'

I gulp, I shake my head. 'No, I don't remember that. I was just a child.'

'You don't?' He looks confused.

I sigh. 'What do you want me to say? You know I mentioned him before. He was one of my parents' friends. He was thin, good head of hair but couldn't hold his drink, came to visit my father from time to time. They got along well. He was only over for a few years so he could return home to Inverness and support his parents' farm.'

'You seem to remember quite a bit about him. How often did he come to your house?'

'I don't know, once a month.' I'm lying. He came every week, not just on the weekends but he would cycle up the dirt road every Thursday and join my father and mother for dinner. 'My father would always try and get him drunk, like it was a game. My father teased him said he wasn't a real Scot, couldn't hold his liquor. One Christmas he brought us pudding, he had made it himself, spent months pouring brandy over it. My father, drunk, poured too much whisky on it, and it burned like a fire in the jungle. He was a nice man, too nice for my father.'

'What did your father and he talk about?'

'Mostly the workers, the price of rubber, the rise of the Chinese gangs, the arrival of the news, stuff like that.'

'And your mother?'

'She would eat and then leave them. She didn't drink much; she only drank when Herbert Scales came around.'

'Herbert Scales?'

'Yes.'

'That is another man on the list.'

I sit forward. 'How many men do you have on this list?'

'Fourteen.'

I swallow. Fourteen, that wasn't right, there were more. Jimmy said there were at least twenty. *Twenty men killed, Philip!* I look at Doctor Lin not knowing whether I said that out loud. I am hoping I didn't. He'll know then, he'll know I remember more.

'Herbert Scales was shot in the head driving home on his

bicycle after visiting the bank on a Friday.'

'Yes, that is right. I remember that. My mother was devastated.'

'What do you remember?'

'Only that he was killed, robbed on his way home. Money was gone and his watch. My mother was very upset, she cried for hours. Amah told her to hush, that she was attracting the demons.'

'Do you know sometime later Herbert Scales' wallet and watch were found?'

'Found?'

'Yes. Funnily enough they had been hidden underneath a tree branch very close to where his body was found.'

'Oh.'

'They were found by a Tamil worker. He saw the watch shining in the light, that is what it reads in the report I found.' He holds up a piece of paper. It is copied; I can't see it clearly.

'Well, he probably did it, the Tamil worker. My father said you always had to watch them, be on your guard, those tappers were only two steps away from robbing you and cutting your throat.'

'No, he didn't, you see he took the watch to the police station and the police officer realised that it was Herbert Scales' missing watch. It had a very distinct look about it, triangular.' He shows me a hand-drawn picture of it.

'So, the police were naturally very concerned. The Tamil worker took them to where he found the watch to help prove his innocence. The police searched and then they found the wallet of Herbert Scales. The wallet is full of old bank notes, he wasn't robbed after all.'

I move in my seat, there is something about the way in which he is looking at me. I see it again, by his feet, orange fur, a mouse, a rat.

'Do you remember anything about this?'

'No, I don't.' I shake my head. 'I was only a child. I wish I did know more. I could have helped out ...'

He cuts me off, 'You said your mother enjoyed the company of Herbert Scales?'

'Yes, it was the only time she drank.'

'Did she know him, I mean before she moved to the Straits?'

'I'm not sure, perhaps, I can't recall.'

'Did you know that Herbert Scales and your mother were once supposed to be married?'

I look at him. 'How do you know that?'

'It's in the archive.' He points to a small notice as he passes it over to me.

It is so tiny I can hardly read it.

The wedding of engineer Herbert James Scales to Mary Elizabeth Mckenna is due to take place Friday afternoon at ...

'But that could be another Mckenna.'

He reads aloud, 'the couple will set sail for Singapore the day afterwards.'

'What is all this? What are you after?' I'm getting angry now. 'This is silly, you are bringing up things that should never be discussed.'

'They shouldn't be? The list of fourteen men murdered shouldn't be discussed? Someone back then thought it was important enough to make a list. Perhaps these murders are connected? You already mentioned Geoffrey Gallagher, that he was shot by a Chinese gang.'

'He was!'

'Well, why is he on this list?'

I shake my head. 'Listen, this is a police matter.'

'I know but I thought perhaps you would like to discuss what happened; whether you remembered everything before I send all my findings to the police.'

'They wouldn't be able to investigate it, everyone involved is dead and all the evidence is gone.' He stares at me curiously and for a moment I believe he thinks I had something to do with this. 'Listen, if you think that I had anything to do with this, I was just a child.'

'I know but you knew every one of these fourteen men, didn't you?' He hands me the list.

I don't want to look at it. I am about to say I'm tired. We are done. I have done my bit for Singaporean history, I just want to be left alone.

'Jimmy,' he suddenly says, 'Jimmy.'

I look up at him. 'What? Who is Jimmy?'

'Your brother?'

'Oh yes, yes of course, what about him?'

'Can we talk about him?'

'There is nothing to be said about him. He died when I was ten. It was an accident.'

'An accident?'

'Yes, he had been struggling for a while.' *A gun shot that vibrated through the house.*

'Suicide?'

I look at the tape recorder. I don't want this on record. I find that my normal strong voice eludes me from time to time since my fall. That voice is powerful, demands to be listened to. I clear my throat and find it again, 'I don't wish to talk about it.'

He bends over and stops the tape and mutters an apology. 'I understand, Mr Philip, I meant no disrespect.'

I am furious. 'Doctor Lin, my brother.' I am breathing heavily, I don't remember the last time I was this angry. 'Jimmy understood things well beyond his years and I don't know what you are hoping to accomplish with this list. These deaths occurred over eighty years ago, they have little relevance today.'

'The past belongs in the past, isn't that so, Wilfred?'

'What did you just say?'

'The ending to your last novel, Mr Philip, the past belongs in the past.' He smiles.

I stare at him enraged; words rush around my head, but I stumble to grab onto any of them. I used to be so good at comebacks, at attacking people verbally, now I am clumsy, muted. I open my mouth, but nothing comes out.

Doctor Lin looks away almost shamefully. I see something again by his feet, something moving, something orange with fur, like a tail of a tiger. He doesn't meet my stare. Finally, I speak. 'I think we should stop for the day, don't you?'

'Of course.' He gets up and I turn my head away from him. He leaves something on the table.

'What is that?'

'The list I found in the archive. A list of all the plantation managers that were killed between 1912 -1925. There are sixteen men on that list.'

'You said fourteen.'

'Angus Sinclair is one of them, his name is circled, and your brother, that is his name there in the corner.' He retraces his steps picks it up and passes it to me. I look at my brother's name, it says James Goundry.

I look down. 'Where has this come from, Doctor Lin?' Philip! What are you doing? It isn't finished. Jimmy pushes me outside the room and slams the door.

'As I said, it was found amongst the possessions of the former police station in Kedah. It seems that someone carefully investigated all of this and left it for someone to come along and find it, or someone hid it. It was just sitting there waiting to be uncovered.'

'You should hand it over to the police, you shouldn't be wasting it on me.'

'Please look at it.'

'No, I don't want to.'

'I think it would help.'

'Help what?'

'Help your memory.'

'My memory? There is nothing wrong with my memory.' I am annoyed. He is insulting me. 'There is nothing wrong with my memory. I remember my first phone number. I remember what colour dress my mother was wearing when she left us that evening. I remember my first taste of ice cream and chewing bubble gum. There is nothing wrong with my memory.'

'Please, Mr Philip, please take a look.'

I grab my glasses and put them on. I stare down at the page and then I see it, my brother's writing. I remember him ruling the lines, I remember him staying up all night and squinting as he tried to write down as much as he could. It was as if he was racing against time. *We have to figure out what is happening, Philip, it is the only way we can make them stop. We need to finish it.*

I look up at him, I am afraid. 'My brother.'

'What?' He leans forward.

'My brother wrote this list. He wanted to be a detective like Sherlock Holmes, he made notes of everything that was going on.'

'How old was your brother then?'

'Thirteen maybe fourteen. He became obsessed with trying to figure out what was going on.'

I look down again. I see names, dates, I remember Herbert laughing, I remember Charlie stumbling out and I remember him, Angus Sinclair, standing in front of me laughing. He had killed something and was wide- eyed crazed. I remember my father shouting, Red! Get Philip out of here! The gun, the blood and then shoes, shoes of the dead.

'The Red Pied Piper,' I whisper.

'Sorry, what did you say?'

'The Red Pied Piper, that was Jimmy's name for him. He killed them, all of them.'

'Why?'

'I don't know, for a game, for fun.'

He doesn't reply.

'My brother knew it. He would stay up and watch and listen to them. I remember one time I saw him and Angus just outside my room. Angus threatened him, said he would put a curse on him to stop him from talking. He would silence me, and I would end up where my mother was, walking through the jungle at midnight, dead, searching for a home that was no longer there.' I stop and let tears fall down from my face.

'I think he killed my brother, Jimmy.' I gasp for air. 'I think he found out that Jimmy had made the list and he shot him.' My heart starts to beat, I want to be sick but there is nothing in my stomach. I lean forward and roar in silence, saliva drips down my chin.

He stops the tape and comes over to me. He sits close to me, and I hear him breathing. His hand goes to my back. 'Breathe,' he says, but I don't want to, I want to die, like Jimmy.

'It should have been me,' I suddenly say, 'I should have been killed.'

Doctor Lin pulls down on the blue rope.

Tom carries me into bed. I am shaking. I can't control it. Jimmy killed. Memories aren't kind to those that ignore them. No wonder I stayed away from all of this, no wonder I never went back to Kedah. Michelle wants to give me a pill but I shake my head, sleep I whisper and so I fall asleep in a state of numbness.

Monday Afternoon

I awaken to him in the room. He is sitting in the corner, reading through his notes. 'You are still here?' My voice croaks.

'Yes. I thought I would stay and make sure you're okay.'

'I see.' I sit up. There is something about the way he is looking at me. What is it now?

He answers without me speaking, 'There are mentions of the myth of the Red Pied Piper in the papers.'

'What papers?'

'Old papers from that time.'

'There are?'

'Yes, like someone is playing a game. Initially I thought it was some inside joke in the papers, but I guess that isn't the case. He became an urban myth, I was told by the locals; they used to tell their sons to be careful, be wary of the white man, he could be the Red Piper.'

'I didn't know that.'

'I'm sure I mentioned it to you before. Did he play a pipe?'

'No, he had a flute. It was a proper flute, not some wooden toy; he played well, and it was like the whole jungle would stop and listen. He was very talented. He would play whenever they would come back from the club. I don't know how he ended up out there transporting children. It's funny where people end up, isn't it?'

'His name is in more than one police report. Did other people know about him; about what he was doing?'

'I don't know. Maybe. Everyone pretended to like him but maybe they were all afraid of him. Maybe they all knew what he had done. What he was capable of.'

'Can you tell me what you remember about him. You said he didn't like young girls, what did you mean?'

'He liked young boys.'

He puts his head down. I say, 'not me, he liked young local boys. He employed two to work with him, when they reached seventeen he would get rid of them and get another two, they were young.'

'How did you know for sure he liked young boys?'

'A feeling, the way his eyes would follow them, instinct.' I shake out my head. 'I am tired.' I say it thinking I am in control but I am not, my voice sounds like a squeal, a cry and he looks at me alarmed.

'I can come back tomorrow.' He gets up and I see it, his tail, a large thick orange tail with black stripes, it's the same as a tiger. It flicks back and forth as he stands still looking at me.

I start to cry. 'Please no, no more, please let me be.'

'I will leave you for now, Mr Philip.'

'No please, I don't want to be left alone. Someone is coming.'

'No one is coming, you are safe here, nothing will happen.'

I start to sob, 'You don't understand.'

'I do, you need to rest.'

'I can't, he will find me.'

'Please, Mr Philip, he won't, he is dead.'

'Maybe he isn't. Maybe he is like what the children say and he is the red man in the jungle still waiting for me.'

'Waiting for you?'

'He asked me to meet him one day and I didn't.'

'Who did?'

'Angus.'

'Why didn't you go?'

'I was scared. Please don't go.' He sits back down. It is getting late. I hear singing outside. Soft singing and I try to stand up. 'Someone is coming,' I say. 'Someone is close.' His tail twitches from side to side.

'What did he want from you?'

'I can't remember. The message came from one of his boys, it was six months after the death of Jimmy. My father had gone to Singapore on business, I was alone in the house.'

'What did you do?'

'I hid with my father's shotgun and waited for him to come and find me but he didn't. I didn't see him in the house after that. He stopped coming. I assumed he was dead. Eventually I left. I was fourteen, my father told me he was sending me back to England and so I went to Singapore and took a steamer back to a home that I did not know.'

'What about your father?'

'He died about six years later of fever. The plantation was then sold in a boom period, and I received the money. It kept me in schools. I moved on, made friends, tried not to think about what had happened.'

'Did your father ever try and contact you?'

I shake my head. 'No, I wrote to him sometimes, sent him school reports. But he never wrote back. One day I got a letter saying he set up a bank account for me, that all would go through a lawyer in London, that there was no need for any future correspondence. That was the last time I heard from him. I never expected a reply and there wasn't any. It was like we had made a silent agreement to never speak again.'

'No external family?'

'No.'

'Did you ever see him again?'

'The leaves,' I suddenly say. 'Look at the floor, see the leaves.'

He looks down and sees them.

'We have to follow them. Come on.' We walk out of my room and through the hallway. We are now outside, and it is bright and hot. He is now a tiger walking in front of me. We follow the trail towards the old, abandoned house.

Sounds in the distance of chisel scraping away at the trees; the smell of fresh rubber as it flows gently out like blood from a deep cut. A trail of leaves folded, left like breadcrumbs, folded by human hands, the trail straight and long, we follow it; Jimmy picks them up as we walk.

'It's like Hansel and Gretel, don't pick them up Jimmy or we won't be able to find our way home.'

We reach the abandoned house, paint peeling from its sides. Hollow window frames, the front door ajar. The tiger looks at me.

'I don't want to go inside.'

He nods and I follow him around the house.

There she is, the girl sitting on the step, a tall stack of leaves next to her, she was making the trail for us.

'You made these?' I say.

'Yes.' She is toothless. There are clothes drying to the side. Women's underclothes, too large for her.

'You can't be here,' I say, 'this is our land.'

'This is not your land,' she hisses. 'This land belongs to no one, not even your father.'

I step back, the tiger moves and I follow him. An enormous python is heading towards us.

She cackles, 'You are scared?'

'No,' I say.

'You should be scared but not of that.'

'What should we be scared of?'

'You will see, it is coming for you.'

'What is?'

'The devil. He comes for the children of those that cross him.'

'Who has crossed him?'

She laughs again.

Tuesday Morning

I waken in a sweat.

'Morning, Philip. How did you sleep?' Tom asks.

'Good, I think.' I stay in bed and watch Tom open the curtains. The sheets up around my neck.

I'm scared. 'The tiger, where did he go?'

'What tiger? The tiger you saw as a child, Philip?'

I nod.

'Did you dream about it?'

I nod. He takes my temperature. 'Well, that's nice. Sit up please. I need to listen to your heart.'

I look out at the day, blue skies, no clouds and pink roses. A door bangs and I jump. 'Someone is coming.'

'You all right, Philip?'

'Is he coming back?'

'Who?'

'The man is he coming?'

'Yes, I think so. It says on the roster. Will be nice for you to talk about your childhood, won't it?'

I don't answer him. He leaves me my breakfast. I sit up and take the notebook.

Tuesday Afternoon

Doctor Lin enters. He drags a chair across; I check for a tail but there isn't one, he must be hiding it. He conceals things well.

'How are you feeling, Mr Philip?'

'Yes, much better.'

He starts the tape recorder. 'Interview with Mr Philip Goundry. Accession Number 3351. Reel One. I have some things to show you if you don't mind. I think they might interest you.' He pulls out a large file and opens it. It contains photographs, old papers. He lays them out on a small side table for me to see. I look down at them. Some of them are of trees close up, some show endless rows of rubber trees. Tappers lined up against the side of a hut, they appear tired, underfed. There is one with men in some sort of uniform leaning up against a bullock cart, they are smiling. I bend over and squint at them, trying to recognise them.

'Do you remember any of these people? These photographs were taken around the time you were living at the plantation.'

'I don't.' I shake my head but then I see the mark on the tree. I sit back, the strange triangle mark on the tree, behind them. Something to do with a gang, robbers leaving their marks. 'That mark,' I say, 'it was made by Chinese gangs; they marked the trees as a warning sign, they all had different meanings.'

'Chinese gangs?'

'Yes.'

'I see.'

He pulls out more pictures, more markings, all similar and then I see the cuts on the trees. The point where they penetrated, the white ooze, dripping down. I think trees can't scream or maybe they could and we just didn't listen. I see another photograph and gently point to it. 'That is my father standing on the veranda next to a man.' I look at the man and gulp. 'He was a murderer.' I whisper it frowning.

'Yes, you said last time, Angus Sinclair.'

'Last time?'

'Yes, Mr Philip, you don't remember the Red Pied Piper? We talked about him last time.'

I shake my head. Last time? Red beard, red hair, red face. I promised myself to remain quiet about him. I can't remember who I promised now, it was so long ago.

He says, 'Can you repeat that?'

'He was a murderer.'

'Yes, you said that last time.'

'He murdered many people. Other plantation managers.

He liked it, killing people, getting away with it, it was all a game to him. I know what he did, I know who he killed'.

'You mean the list?'

'Oh, Jimmy's list! Yes. Jimmy knew, Jimmy knew everything. He told me I was too young to know; he said that I had to swear on mummy's life, and I did, I swore not to tell anyone. But Jimmy, he was so smart, he made the list; he knew what they were doing. He listened to everyone, he wrote down the names, he heard everything. He knew that they shot them and left them for dead.'

'They? Who?'

'Because they could. Amah said he was the devil himself. Sometimes she used to hide us whenever he came over; lock us up in our rooms.'

He looks at me surprised. He eyes the tape; I am almost expecting him to stop it.

'It's okay,' I say, 'maybe you don't want to hear it.'

'No,' he shakes his head, 'no, I do want to hear it. Please continue.'

'He was friends with my father. Good friends. They had an agreement.'

'What kind of agreement?'

'Well, to kill other plantation managers, well that for starters ...'

'Your father?' He looks shocked. 'He was also involved.

But why?'

'To get rid of the competition I suppose. I don't know for sure and then they moved on to other things.'

'Other things?'

'Getting and selling the girls. Once they were used up, they would dump them back outside the convents.'

'What?'

'Young girls, younger than me.'

'What?'

'Jimmy figured it out. I'm sure it's all there in the records if you know what you are looking for. We didn't have journalists like we have today. Most of the time they were inexperienced. Sometimes they were bored women wanting to write about parties and lunches; some gossip but mostly about who was sleeping with whom. They weren't concerned with young kids being prostitutes and about killings.'

He shakes his head. 'I don't understand. You knew all along?'

'I didn't know, not really. Or, well, I had forgotten. It was hard as a child to understand what they were doing but Jimmy figured it out. Now when I think back to it, I'm sure it was the heat that got to everyone; dulled some of them down and to some others it poked them, tore off their façade, their primal urges unleashed, lust, jealousy, rage. It made people do things; crazy things to feel better. Jimmy wrote the list, but he wrote other things as well.'

'What other things?'

'Detailed reports, I think. I don't know where they are now.' Philp stop looking at it, you shouldn't read it, you're better off not knowing. Jimmy's voice; it's so clear as if he is sitting right next to me.

'How do you know all this? You haven't mentioned any of this before.' He leans forward and looks confused.

My mind is clear now, the dreams and memories are starting to line up in order like the rubber trees planted eighteen feet apart, cultivated and ready to bleed white latex.

'I remember I found out the real story when I was about twenty. A young man came to see me when I was at Cambridge, he told me about what had happened, about who my father really was. He said that he worked at the plantation after I left. He knew that my father was trafficking girls with Angus Sinclair; that they had started doing it during a tough period to make money. He mentioned sacks of money that they used to hide in the outhouses. Money that they had received. I remember I saw one, one day; I thought it was seeds but it was light, and I untied it. It was filled with cash and jewellery, watches, rings, necklaces, that sort of thing. The man told me about what he had done and him ...' I point to Angus' face on the photograph, 'how he was the devil we had feared as children. You know Angus' voice was abnormally high, you never would think he was capable but that is the thing about the devil, Doctor Lin, he never comes in the form you would think.'

Doctor Lin goes to speak but I won't let him, I keep on speaking fast. 'I don't know why my father got involved with him, I can only think that he would have threatened him. I don't like to think of my father as a bad man, but I do think he did those things and he helped Angus. You never want to believe that your parents are villains because if they are what does that make you?'

Doctor Lin puts his head down. He looks sad. I have taken him away from what he wanted.

I say, 'I guess plantation life wasn't easy for anyone.'

He looks up almost defeated.

'It made people do things that they wouldn't have done before.' He doesn't answer me.

It is true that once you start tapping the rubber tree, the latex starts to stream out slowly, carefully like my memories. I speak before I think. 'You know I did see him again – Angus.' I speak fast trying to keep up with the memory.

'One evening in Singapore after the war, I had returned and was working for R. S. Tyrone Shipping, I went into a bar on Hong Kong Street. Angus was sitting with a young boy and drinking whisky. I didn't think he knew me and so I rushed past him and went inside searching for a friend I was due to meet. Suddenly I heard him laugh.

Is that you? Kid? How are you? Look at you now, look how big you have gotten, the image of your father. I'd know you anywhere. I remember shaking as his hands grabbed hold of my shoulders. I looked around and calmly told myself that he wouldn't do anything, there were too many people around. I asked, how are you, Angus?

Can't complain, business all but dried up after the rubber crash but still can't complain. I'm now working on the shipyard helping to offload cargo, hard work but very profitable if you can imagine it.

He was happy, almost jovial. It was unsettling. He said, I never got to say how sorry I was to hear about your father, he was such a good man. I remember I snorted but he didn't seem to notice. I think I mumbled something to the effect of yes, thank you. He tried to buy me a drink, get me to join him and his boy but I declined. The person I was supposed to meet was still not there and so I left and promised him that I would come by and see him at the docks. I remember he grabbed my hand as I started to walk away and he said something very odd to me, he said, I sure miss the old days, don't you? There was some good hunting back then, wasn't there? He grinned at me and winked.

I walked away without answering and headed up the road hoping to meet my friend. He was there getting out of a cab, I told him to get back in. I said there was an old girlfriend in the bar that I didn't want to see and he believed me.

After that I started working long days at the port but I remember now that I saw him once more. Angus. I was monitoring some cargo that was coming in from China. He hadn't changed much since I saw him in the bar, he was shouting over to the locals to check papers and then he saw me, he hobbled over grinning.

He said, well if it isn't Master Goundry. How are you?

I'm well, thank you.

What are you wearing? A suit? That doesn't fit you very well, does it?

You don't think so?

No, I don't. I don't know what your father would have made of it.

It was then I looked at him in the heat of the day and asked him out right, what happened to my mother?

He stood back and swallowed hard, his eyes grew large, and he shook his head. I don't know what you are talking about.

But you do. I found her suitcase a week later in the jungle.

She must have dropped it when she was running away. She must have not needed any of it, her fancy man must have told her to leave everything behind, he was rich you know.

He was? What was his name?

Oh, I forget now, Richards, Rogers, something with an R. Did you know him?

Yes, I knew him, we all knew him, he was the district officer. He had only been there a month when he ran off with your mum.

I don't remember him.

You don't? Nice looking chap, tall, thin, elegant ways about him. He drove that fancy navy car.

I see. I don't recall anyone like that, and I didn't then. I don't recall the district officer going missing around the same time. Was he our district officer?

Yes, yes he was. Shame really, he arrived with great intentions, he wanted to modernise everything. He was all for mixing the locals and our kind better, he wanted better pay for the locals, better living conditions and all that. He stopped speaking and stared out towards the sea, a ship that had just left honked its horn signalling its departure. It was like he was trying to avoid speaking to me.

So, the district officer met my mother and gave up everything?

Well, I don't know for sure, I wasn't around then. I was up north for the first two weeks dropping off the girls, but I remember when I came back your father was in a state about her and this new district officer, he said that they had been seen together, and have taken to walking in the evenings together on the outskirts of the jungle.

Did he confront her?

Yes, I suppose he did, I can't remember now lad, I'm sorry. But there was such gossip about it all.

Funny I don't remember any of it.

No but you were just a boy.

Maybe but I knew most other things that were going on.

Did you now? He looked me up and down, so you knew what was going on, did you?

I stood firm and looked at him, I knew everything.

He smirked. Your father in a dress?

I nod.

But you don't remember about her, do you?

My mother?

So, you don't know everything, Mr Suit.

I cleared my throat. It is a shame that you don't recall the district officer's name. I would very much like to know it.

Why?

Well, perhaps he is alive?

He looked away. Perhaps, you can always check the records, maybe you can find his name in there.

1920?

Umm, yes I suppose it was, how time moves on. He laughed and moved away from me. I better go, I have to see someone about the next shipment. He smiled and walked away, but then he stopped and turned. Richardson, William Richardson. Check the records, he went missing in 1920.

Missing? But you said he left.

He did. The very same night as your mother. At least she took a suitcase. He took nothing; the lamp was still burning when they checked the house, and a book was left half open on a table.

A book?

Francis Bacon, I believe.

How do you remember that?

Because I helped search Richardson's home, your father and brother did to.

My brother?

Aye, your brother. Poor kid, he said sadly. He then got up and walked away in between the crates and boxes. I never saw him again after that.

The thing is I don't remember Richardson. He never came to our home; I never knew of him. I enquired in the old record office that was close to the customs house. He went missing after a month; they actually suspected a tiger had taken him as there was no sign of foul play, no weapon found or missing, no footprints, nothing, only his lamp burning. His money and possessions were all there. I asked for the records of my mother, it just said she was missing, no police report, nothing. I thought about pursuing it, going after both of them.

My mother's disappearance was never officially reported on, it was either forgotten or hushed up, it was like she didn't even exist. There were times throughout the years when I began to question whether she did exist or whether I imagined her.'

Wednesday Morning

I nod politely as he enters, he doesn't return it. He doesn't meet my eyes until he starts to record. He speaks, 'Accession number 3551. Reel one.'

He mentions the dates I lived there, my residency and then he mentions my father. That I am the son.

'Can we discuss your father?'

He doesn't smile like he used to – warm, friendly, encouraging – he looks at me as if he is scared.

'Yes, we can talk about him.'

'So, your father was the manager of Cullodena Plantation.'

'Yes, that is right.'

'Last time we discussed his relationship to this man Angus Sinclair seen in this photograph. Item 2304.' He places it down again in front of me, I look at it. I'm not afraid anymore.

'Yes, that's right.'

'Can you talk a bit more about their relationship?'

'What do you want to know?'

'You mentioned money last time we spoke, that money was exchanged, you said you saw a big sack of money in one of the outhouses.'

I swallow. I glance down at the photograph. I remember my father, how he grabbed the back of my neck. Stop crying, she can't hear you, when you're dead you're dead, that's it. He squeezed harder. Stop crying, he leaned in and whispered in my ear, or else I'll give you something to cry about boy.

'Yes,' I try and smile. 'Yes, they did business together, well if you can call it that.'

'What kind of business was it again?'

I clear my throat and reach for the water. He gets up and helps me. He doesn't smell of anything today. I take a sip; my hands are shaking. My father's voice: when you're dead you're dead. There is no harm. No one is coming.

'They ran girls together.'

That rattles him, he looks at me surprised. 'You mentioned that last time. Could you be more specific?'

'Yes, young girls. Once a year Angus Sinclair would come and take a group of them out of the convent. He said he was delivering them to the outposts around the Straits. He had a list of families that needed cheap domestic help and for the exchange of about fifteen girls the convent would get a load of money. He would reuse this list; tell them he needed more girls but then sell them on for his own gain. They used to call him Red, the other managers, you know after his red beard. I assume everyone knew what he was doing.'

'I found more mentions of the Red Pied Piper in the

papers, in the "Topics of to-day" gossip column of the *Malaya Tribune*.' He clears his throat. 'What did he do with the girls?'

I shake my head and feel a twitch in my side. 'He rented them out, for an hour, a day, a week. Mostly to lonely workers. Sometimes he would take them to brothels in Penang or KL, sell them to the owners.'

He sits back and looks at the tape recorder. 'How do you know this?'

'I think I always knew it. Jimmy told me he made a list, that everything had been written down on it. He made reports. But then there was a fire at our bungalow just before I left for school. Everything was destroyed. It was that man in Cambridge who came to see me who confirmed everything.'

Doctor Lin is quiet.

'It was a different time. The police force was non-existent and those that were there spent most of their time running around after the Chinese gangs. It was easy to hide, even in broad daylight. No one was watching, not really.'

And then I say it. 'People got away with a lot more.'

'Like what?'

'Like murder.'

'Murder?'

'Yes.'

'You mean the Chinese gangs? And Red and your father?'

'And others.'

'What others? Locals?'

'Them as well.'

'Why would they murder? For money?'

'Yes, among other things. It's easy to murder in the jungle, it's too hot, bodies can't sit for too long, evidence was never taken. You see bodies were buried quickly. There was a small write-up in the newspapers, just a paragraph about their passing, limited details of their death. Sometimes they claimed it was suicide but most of the time it wasn't, it was something else, greed, envy, lust. And then there is him.'

I look down at the photograph, his red beard. 'I remember his bracelets, the deep scars on his face. The Red Pied Piper. A nickname given to him by Jimmy. Everyone laughed but it was true, the children, the flute and his red beard. Look here he comes, the mighty Red Pied Piper! The rest of them laughed, my father laughed the loudest.'

'The man you called the devil.'

'I did? When?'

'Last time we spoke.'

'Huh.'

Wednesday Afternoon

'Sometimes strong breezes would rush through the plantation; they would whoosh through without any reason. Amah would say, someone is coming, someone is on their way. She said the land was always telling us things only we didn't listen hard enough. One time I laid down and placed my ear to the ground. I said, I am listening, I can hear you.'

He laughs.

'All I could hear was the blood in my ear going round and round. Another time I tried to talk to the trees. I stood and watched them. Rubber trees don't move a whole lot and one day I sat and watched the tapper and the latex dripping. It made me feel sick as if the tree was bleeding to death. I ran home in tears, locked myself in my room and never told anyone what happened.'

I laugh, 'It's funny what you do as a kid, what scares you and what you remember.'

He grins and nods. He says, 'When I was a kid I was petrified of aliens coming to get me. I used to barricade my bedroom with cushions so they couldn't come in. Every morning I would check my skin for marks in case they planted a secret chip on me.' He shakes his head. 'It is silly now but when I was a child I really believed that they would come and get me.'

I laugh. 'That is strange.'

He is laughing and nodding. 'Please, Mr Philip, continue.'

Where was I? 'My mother had a small rose garden that she tried in vain to keep flourishing but it's blooms would vary year to year, some years the roses would just poke out their small heads, other years they would flourish and there would be a great abundance of them. She watered them the same, made the cook save eggshells that she scattered around their roots. Yet some years they only gave out small buds that didn't open but laid closed tight like unripe nuts.'

'Do you think that Herbert Scales came out looking for your mother?'

'I don't know, perhaps. It's strange to think that they were once engaged. It never bothered my father that he was around. I guess it was nice to have people visiting, also for them. People get lonely in the jungle.'

'Was he married?'

'No, I don't think so. I don't remember a wife.'

'Did they often talk about home?'

'Yes, of course they did. I didn't like it when they did, so I never paid much attention to that.'

'Thank you again for agreeing to contribute to this.'

He leaves. I'm so tired I don't even say goodbye. I watch the roses bob up and down in the sunlight as if they are dancing. Roses in our garden, petite pink roses that my mother tried to keep alive, roses that the staff overwatered, then underwatered; they were so delicate and foreign to their eyes.

Wednesday Evening

I write in my notebook:

Noises in the jungle almost human, singing heard from miles away. Flute notes. Shouts, whispers, sound of footprints that had no body attached to them. Light burning in the distance. Trees standing still. Trees that bleed latex. Trees that emitted foul smelling goo; trees that watched and waited. Trees that didn't protect but were a victim to our hands. When I moved to England, I realised that sometimes trees do protect, that some are their own master.

The first few years back I lied and said my family was alive. I told people they were rich, successful. I made up stories that Jimmy was working with my father and the reason I didn't return was because they were worried about me getting the fever.

I quickly learned on the steamer ship home that I wasn't special. I needed to change my accent. I had been made fun of by the customs officer. Jock off home, eh? he said. Plenty where you came from, son.

I watched and studied the other men. I quickly made up a new version of myself, one that allowed me to move on. I took on other people's lives to cover the shame of my own.

You know I don't think even now that my father was a bad man. I just think the jungle took something away from him, some sort of protection, the jungle stole that from him and he was left almost naked, his full self gone, shredded like the bark of the tree. I don't know why he agreed to join Red. Perhaps boredom, perhaps Red knew about my father and his dressing and blackmailed him. I don't know for sure. I only know that I knew I would never return. I would never see him again.

I never drank like my father, I never gambled, I always stayed away from men like Angus Sinclair. I tried to avoid all the things that I associated with my father. I married once, had one child and then lived alone. I didn't want to test myself by having another relationship. Sure, I had women off and on but always at a distance. I was careful to conceal emotions. Sex was an act, like eating succulent dark chocolate, something to be enjoyed on occasion but not often. I suppose none of us ever want to repeat the sins of our parents. We spend most of our life trying not to be like them and then we find out we are exactly the same, and sometimes we discover we are worse. My boy I sent away young to school. I saw him rarely and before I knew it, he had married young and had multiple children. He bought a small farm in Scotland where his family breeds pedigree dogs. It's funny how that stayed within the family. Despite my intentions, he owned a large farm, his family not as isolated as our plantation but they returned to the homeland of my father; a homeland I have always avoided. I suppose for most of my life I avoided anything to do with my father, with our life in Malaya and I avoided my son for having the same look as my father, one that was proud, friendly and strong. I looked like my grandmother, they often said. A grandmother I had never met and when I used to stare into my face I searched for this grandmother, but she never seemed to find me. A wicked streak she had, my mother said once when I asked about her, but you don't have that, Philip, you are like a ray of sunshine compared to her. Is she dead? I don't know, perhaps. She would change the subject and I would forget to ask further.

It's funny how my parents seemed to be running away from something and it seemed to catch up with them anyway. Memories are odd things, sometimes they creep up on you like a tiny insect brushing against your skin, you look down and there you see the creature climbing up, you watch it with interest and then flick it away, it is useless. Other times you hear a voice, a voice calling you, and you turn, a voice from someone and you stop and take a breath, who was that? What do they want? A colour, a flower, a smell, a slight breeze, a door shutting. Small normal things that can bring something back. I had been good about suppressing memories, there was no use for them. I was never one to sit back in a chair and replay events that had happened to me, I would rather replay other lives. There was so much else that I could think of. It is strange to be looking back now.

I hear Tom walking around outside. 'Tom?'

He walks in. 'Finished, have you? You looked so engrossed I didn't want to disturb you.'

I sigh and sit back. 'I am finished for now. Thank you.'

'Is it easy?' he asks. 'You know, making up stories.'

'Oh, this isn't a story but yes it was easy for me.'

He laughs, 'Yeah, I guess we tell ourselves the stories we want to be told, don't we? Like I tell myself I am twelve stone, and I should have that extra slice of carrot cake, but you and I both know I am closer to fourteen stone, and I should only be eating the carrot and not the cake.' He chuckles and I smile.

'We do what we have to, to survive.'

'Yeah, I guess you're right. It's past ten, you better get yourself ready for bed. I'll bring you in your tea.'

'Thank you, Tom.'

Wednesday Night

I awake crying. Michelle is holding my hand. She looks concerned. 'I'm sorry, another dream.'

'It's fine,' she says, 'you were calling out for your mother.'

'I was?' My face is still wet with tears. I was. I miss her. I start to quietly sob; it hurts to cry, and I can't control it.

Michelle sits with me and tells me, 'It's okay, let it out.'

Tom enters with a syringe, he pushes it into my arm. They both looked concerned.

'We can cancel Doctor Lin if you want, Philip. He doesn't have to come.'

I shake my head. 'Memories can only be suppressed for so long. I need to finish it. I need it to end.'

Michelle gently touches my forehead, 'If you're sure?'

I nod. 'It's my subconscious that is having the problem.'

She smiles. 'I know but maybe it's not right to go back so far.'

'It's too late for that now. I just have a hard time remembering what is real and what isn't. I begin to think I imagined it all but then he comes with files. Jimmy's handwriting, lists of names of people that I used to know but haven't remembered for years.'

'Like your mother?'

I look at Michelle, there is something about the way she says it that makes me feel uneasy.

'Yes, things about my mother. Did I say something?' I ask suddenly afraid.

'You said you were sorry you killed her.'

I turn my face away from her and look up at the ceiling. Someone is coming, someone is coming, she says, my mother in my room sitting on my bed. Someone is coming, they are going to take us away. Don't leave the room no matter what you do, you mustn't leave your room until I come and get you, then we will wake your brother. We will go and we will be safe. You be a good boy; I just need to get our things from outside.

Thursday Morning

He is eating Madeira cake. I see him eyeing up my piece. He speaks, his mouth full. 'What do you mean by that?'

'I don't know. They went in search of a better life, and maybe they had it for a while but then it fell apart, didn't it? Maybe they were cursed from the beginning'.

He looks at me and sighs. He stops the tape and bows his head. 'Thank you, Mr Philip, it has been a pleasure.'

'Has it?' I look at him surprised, 'Has it really? I don't know what you got out of this.'

'Well, a very valuable insight into growing up on a plantation.'

'I am sure there are others that grew up in more peaceful surroundings.'

'Actually, you are the only one we could find who is living.'

'Oh, am I?'

'Yes.'

'A dying breed.' I laugh.

'Quite.' He giggles like a child.

Thursday Afternoon

'Shall we start?'

I nod at him. It is cold, his hair is wet. I am tired. All I want to do now is sleep. Sleep is the only thing that mutes everything.

He sees my arm; it is bruised from the injections. My hand starts to shake, and he reaches for the glass before I can touch it. 'Here,' he says passing it to me. I take it and nod, grateful.

'How are you? Ready to start?' He asks.

'Yes.' I feel weak, weaker than I was when this started. The tiger is coming for me; she is stalking me at night. I can almost feel her breath.

'I am Doctor Lin, and I am speaking to Philip Goundry, accession case 3351, oral testimony, reel one.' He looks around the room as if he is expecting someone else to be there with us. He sits down opposite me. 'I found some maps.'

'Maps?'

'Maps of the locations of all the plantations. Maps of your area.'

'Oh, I see.'

He takes out the maps. Maps made by one of the workers.

A map made around the time my father first purchased the land. Maps filled with numbers, odd-shaped blocks.

I say, 'I have never seen this before.'

'You haven't? They made it to keep a track of land ownership, I suppose.'

I see. My eyes scan over it, I try and look for our plot. He points, 'Here, that is where you lived.'

I look down, a badly drawn rectangle, boundary lines. I see and I point to the two small triangles, 'Were they the mountains?'

He leans over. 'Yes.' He nods, 'Yes. Were they big mountains?'

'You haven't been there?'

'No, not yet. I hope to go when I return.'

'You should. Two mountains side by side. The sisters are what they called them. I could see them from my bedroom window but they always felt as if they were so far away.'

'Would you like to return?' He says this gently, almost as if he is afraid about how I am going to respond.

'No, I'm too old for that now.'

'Would you have if you were younger?'

I shake my head. I don't answer him.

He pulls out more. 'I made many copies, would you like to see them?'

I nod.

He unrolls them. Their colours are not very strong but I can just make out the lines and territories. 'The jungle is here,' he points to a group of strange signals, 'and this is where you lived. Bungalow number five it reads.'

'Bungalow number five?'

'Yes, they didn't write down the name of the plantations back then, I don't know why.'

'It's because they changed hands too often,' I say. 'It was cheaper to just label things simply then without paying for another man to make a map.'

'I see.'

I look down at the map. It doesn't make any sense to me really, I don't remember the roads, the dirt tracks on this map. I see the D/O house. 'The district officer?'

'Yes, that is his house.'

'Did you ever find out what happened to William Richardson?' I say it surprising myself.

'The district officer that went missing in 1920?'

'Yes. He had only been in the job a month and then he disappeared, at the time they thought a tiger had got him'.

'Can you tell me the month?'

'January or February, just after Christmas.'

He scribbles it down.

'I never met him, someone mentioned it to me a couple of years later.'

'That man that came to see you in Cambridge?'

I look at him shocked, 'How did you know about him?'

'You mentioned him before. Do you remember anything about this man? What he wanted?'

I shake my head. I can feel my body start to react. 'Umm, all I remember is that he was waiting for me outside my college. He needed to talk to me. We went to a pub and he said he knew things, things about my father. He worked with him, that I should pay him ... yes, that was it, he wanted money. I had forgotten that.'

'He wanted to blackmail you?'

'I guess so. I told him he was wasting his time. I had no money. But he said he would tell the police what he had found out.'

'Did he say how he knew?'

'No,' I shake my head. 'He was about my age. Strange. I remember he told me about them running girls. I got up and left after he mentioned he would go to the police.'

'What happened then?'

'Umm. I left; I was angry. He grabbed my arm and said to me that the apple doesn't fall far from the tree, does it? I left him and, well, I never heard from him again. That's odd, isn't it? He never contacted me again. I wonder why?'

Doctor Lin shakes his head. 'Maybe he died in the war?'

'Yes, maybe. Strange though. Also, that a D/O would just

go missing.'

He looks at me and takes a deep breath in. 'I know. So, I found something about your mother.'

I sit back. 'Oh yes?'

'Yes, do you mind if I switch this on?'

'Fine.' I'm suddenly afraid of what he is going to say or what he will reveal.

'Ascension number 3351. Reel one. Mr Goundry, your mother's name was Mary Elizabeth Mckenna, is that correct?'

'Yes.'

'She disappeared in 1920, correct?'

'Yes, she did. They said … they said she left.'

'I see. You never heard from her again?'

'No, I didn't.' I suddenly have the urge to bite my nails, something I haven't done since I was a young man.

'Do you know that a body was found in 1935? The bones of a female in the jungle. Her skull indicated that she had been shot in the back of the head.'

'Close range?' I ask.

'No quite a distance. The report is here.'

I take it my hands shaking. 'Where did you find these files?'

'British archives. The British took them home with them when they returned, too much highly sensitive material in them apparently.' He smiles and bends forward, he is excited.

'What do you mean by that?'

'Drug cartels, Chinese gangs, local thieves.'

'I don't remember them finding a body, but in 1935 I was at school over here.'

'Well, they did. There is more.'

'Okay.'

'You mentioned William Richardson?'

'Yes, yes I did.'

'His name is also in that file.' He is watching me carefully now.

'What?' I turn the pages over and see his name.

'He reported her missing.'

'I see.'

'Actually, he also reports that both you and your brother were also missing. Does that strike you as odd?'

'What? Why would he do that. I don't know. I don't know anything about it.' My mother's voice, get ready, Philip, someone is coming. I swallow and stare at the floor.

'You don't recall him?'

'No, as I said before I never met him.'

'He wasn't the district officer.'

'He wasn't?'

'No, he was the police officer in charge of everything in this area.' He points at the map, and circles most of it.

'I see.'

'Who told you he was the district officer?'

'Angus Sinclair.'

'I see.'

'He told me he was part of the search party that he went to his house and the lamp was still on but William Richardson had gone.'

'And the tiger?'

'I don't know why they thought that, perhaps there was a sighting.'

'Was there one around that time, can you remember?'

I close my eyes and I'm in my old bedroom. I'm looking out of the window.

'It's late evening, the light is fading, and I see something moving slowly outside, on all fours, prowling. It is a tiger hunting, heading towards our house. My father has warned me to be on the lookout for them. There have been many sightings in the last week; they are hungry and are coming closer to the houses. I run out of my room hissing for my father, for my brother but there is no one and so I run into my parents' room and take one of my father's rifles. I walk back into my room. Open my window wider and place the rifle on the window frame. I point it towards the creature that is moving slowly, and I shoot. Bang. I hit it, it slumps over and I dash outside to see it. But something stops me, someone is at the door. A man, a tall man, he looks at me curiously, where are you going?

Outside, there is a tiger, I have shot it.

Have you now. He doesn't move, he just stands there and looks at me. I don't move, I don't know why. I can't. There is something about him. He breathes heavily.

Where is your mother?

She went out looking for my father.

When?

Just after dinner.

He looks around the bungalow. The shutters are open to allow the night air to cool down the house.

He stands so quietly as if he is waiting for me to say something, but I don't, I remain silent.

Where did your father go?

Outside with Red, they went in search of the tiger, but I got him, I should tell them. I go to the front door and try and push my way past him but he grabs me roughly and flings me back. He is stronger than he looks.

He says, I don't think that is a good idea.

But they will want to know.

Where is your brother?

In his bedroom sleeping.

Go and wake him will you, tell him to hurry up and come outside.

I don't ask why but I take the rifle from my room and try and stuff it into my shorts and cover it with my shirt. I wake my brother who is sleepy, he looks at me annoyed.

You have to come, I whisper, I killed a tiger.

He gets up and follows me through the house. Outside we go and the tall thin man is standing next to a shorter fatter man. I stand in front of him.

We are friends of your mother's, the shorter man says, his voice is oddly deep.

I giggle but my brother pinches me.

Our mother isn't here, he says.

I know, he said. And your little brother shot a tiger?

Yes, yes, I did.

He smiles. Well, shall we go and have a look at it?

It is just around the back, I say.

We walk around the back and then I see it, it's bright orange, slumped over. I move towards it carefully and then I see underneath the old mango tree, it's not a tiger, it's a human, it has legs, bright burnt orange, the dress my mother had on at dinner.

I fall to my knees and cry.'

I'm crying again and look up at him. 'Did I say all that out loud?' I ask, shivering.

'Yes.' He nods looking at me sadly. He reaches over and grabs the blanket from my bed and places it on me. I am trembling and crying.

'You need something?' he asks. I nod, I point towards the rope, he nods and tugs it once.

Michelle comes running in and looks at him and me. 'What's going on in here? Everything alright?'

I feel her arm on my shoulder, it feels like an electric shock, and I start to jitter.

'Could you move back please, give me some space,' she says to Doctor Lin, and he backs away and stares at me. I can almost see tears in his eyes but I can't be sure. Then I black out.

I am gone for a while in the dark, senses muted. I can't be sure of anything, even who I am, where I am and why I am.

Friday Morning

A door bangs.

I waken not remembering for a moment what happened. My room is clean. The chairs are back to where they should be; it's like no one was ever here. I look around and see the bright sun trying to get through the blackout curtains, it's a warm day I think. I sit up and look towards my chair, my clothes are folded neatly ready for the day ahead. I move towards them and stop, bright orange, not fur but cloth, legs without claws, pale hands, and frizzy red hair, blood from the back.

My father's voice sounds, get away, he fires into the air and the two men turn to him, you did this? He shouts. They don't answer they only look at me.

I start to speak but can't.

Who did this? Who did this? He screams.

I am shaking. I wet myself. My brother answers for me, they did, they did.

Red and my father hold up their guns.

The men start to back away, no, no it was the boy, they say, it was an accident.

You expect me to believe my son would do this, you were

159

after her, you were after her, you have been after her the whole time.

You need to tell us where she is.

Who?

The girl in the house, the girl that you have kept in that house, we found another body this morning.

That wasn't me.

Red looked at my father questioningly.

Mr Goundry, you should come with us. And you, Mr Sinclair. It is over.

My father is shaking. No, no I don't want to. The girl, she wanted to live there, and I let her. I was only letting her do what she wanted.

The man glances over at us. Please, Mr Goundry, for your boys. She wouldn't want this; she wouldn't want you to kill me.

Well, she isn't here now; he looks down at her body.

Don't, this is a mistake.

You are the mistake, Richardson; you have been ever since you arrived. Everything was working smoothly till you turned up. You know they warned me about you, said you were on your way.

Who warned you?

The girl said you ran into some trouble in Singapore; said they needed to get you out.

He shakes his head. I was trying to protect them.

From whom, from me? He laughs.

From those men you get money from.

He gulps and points the gun at him again. I don't know what you are talking about.

You don't know about accepting payment for those men to be with those girls.

No, I don't, and you better shut up. It's not liked those girls minded. They were well paid. It gave them a chance to survive.

I cross my forehead, my tears stop, my father laughs.

It isn't right, Mr Goundry.

Who is to tell me what is right? Huh? You? You were always after her.

No, that's where you are wrong, it was her that came to me about you. Mary took the girl that you kept in the old, abandoned house to see me, she told me everything.

My brother moves closer to me and grabs me.

Richardson looks at us both. You should think about your boys, what this will do to them.

My father looks at us, they will be fine, it's time they learned anyway. Time must have a stop. He then shoots Richardson through the head; the shorter man falls to his knees and Red shoots him. I turn my face into Jimmy's shoulder and I grab onto him tightly.

161

My father looks at me, you better help us out here, take off his shoes for starters.

'I don't remember anything after that, sometimes you witness things that are even too much for your brain. Jimmy suffered after that, he had awful nightmares and wet the bed. He stopped talking to me. I tried to talk to him but he would always turn away. Red took to coming over often the next few months and one time I saw him stroking my brother's knee under a table. A few months later Jimmy was dead, people said it was because he missed my mother.' I sigh.

'We went from being an admired progressive plantation to being one that was almost blacklisted. My father lost workers and found it difficult to hire new ones for a while. I don't really recall the time between these events, it is like it all happened to someone else. There were endless days wasted, me going to the abandoned house searching for the pontianak, hoping she could bring Jimmy back. I started folding banana leaves myself, leaving trails for her, but she never came. My father wouldn't speak to me. He fired all of the house staff the night my mother died. I never got to say goodbye to Amah. She vanished along with everything else I knew.'

'What happened after your brother died?' he asks me. I don't look at him, I don't even know if he is really here.

'I don't remember much. I just remember coming back from checking the tappers' bowls and finding my father on the front steps. He wasn't crying, he was smoking, staring off into the distance. I knew something had happened. What is it? I asked.

Your brother, he is dead. He then got up and went into the house.' I swallow and let tears run down my face, I am sobbing.

'When he died, I was so devastated that I couldn't breathe. I ran out towards the jungle, and I ran until I couldn't stop. I got lost and lay down on the ground. I was ready for the earth to consume me up whole and then I heard it walking. I sat up and saw it coming towards me, the tiger. I stared at it petrified but also willing it to kill me. Instead, it sniffed me; its head butted mine and then it moved on. I cried then, cried like I have never cried before. It had started to get dark and so I stood up and followed it, thinking I ... I would live with it, the tiger. But it took me towards the road and vanished into the jungle and I never saw it again. I stayed for a few years.'

I close my eyes and breathe out. 'That's when I started to realise what my father and Red were really doing. The girls, the money.'

'And Herbert Scales?'

'I believe that Herbert saw my father, you know, in those clothes and he wrote and told my mother. My father killed him in a rage. My father suffered greatly from periods of rage. Anger like you have never seen, almost as if he was possessed.

Nothing or no one could calm him.'

'How long did these periods last?'

'Hours. Broken glasses, smashed plates. That was hard for my mother, she loved having nice things and he would always destroy them first. Drink does a lot of damage,' I say. I look away.

'One time I found him picking out broken splinters of glass from his heel. He looked through me during those times, it was as if none of us existed to him. My mother, I guess she contacted Richardson, to ask for help to get us out. They must have made some sort of plan, that would have happened if it wasn't for me.' I say that and I am numb.

'I see.'

'There weren't enough police back then, people could get away with anything.' I'm shaking. The three side table lights are on, one is starting to flicker. I watch, trying to remember when it got dark. The flicker stops and the lights seems stronger.

'So, Richardson was trying to help you get out?'

'I think so. I'm not sure'.

'Did your father ever remarry?'

I shake my head. 'No. After my mother left no women came to the house. I left at fourteen. I left for school, sailed away. My father died of fever six years later. I never returned to the house. The last time I saw my father was for dinner the night before. He had taken to ignoring me then and so he read the paper while he ate. I went to bed and the next morning I left early. I never saw him again.' I suddenly start laughing. It is odd, as if I have no control over myself.

'What is funny?'

'I just remembered there was women's clothing drying outside. They weren't my mothers. I'm sure they were his. It is sad that he hated that part of himself so much. Sometimes you only want to remember the good things; you know, make out it wasn't so bad.'

'Did you ever tell anyone?'

'Never. There is a certain shame in knowing that you did something, even if you didn't really know.'

He stares at me; he looks sad, almost uncomfortable. 'I think I should go now,' he says.

'I suppose I have to talk about it. It would be a shame if I died and none of this was ever known. I guess this is not the ideal history that you were envisaging.'

'Did your father ever mention it to you afterwards, about you killing your mother?'

I shake my head. 'No, never.' I sigh and let tears stream down my face. 'All these years of avoiding the truth or pretending to be someone else. I never wanted to face it. But I can now, I guess.'

I stare at my notebooks. I point. 'Perhaps someone can take them, and the world can find out who I am and what I did. Wrong the rights of the past and all that.' I look up and see that no one is in here with me. I have been speaking to myself.

Friday Afternoon

He stares at me, the tiger. He is lying on the floor. He yawns and says, 'No and I don't know how much I can use but I will have to give it over to the police.'

'The police?'

'Yes.' He nods solemnly.

'But everyone involved is dead.'

'I know but it's still a crime.'

'I see.'

He stands up and stretches out, a long, feline stretch. His claws scratch the carpet. 'Thank you, Mr Goundry, for your time; on behalf of the Singaporean government we are grateful for your contribution.'

'That's it then.'

The tiger nods.

'I see.'

'You can rest now, Mr Goundry.'

I look at him surprised. 'I think it's too late for that.'

'Sometimes it's good to finally remember.'

'You think? I would have rather continued not knowing.'

'I must be off.'

Michelle walks in, as if she was listening by the side of the door. 'You off now?'

He nods.

I give a little smile. I feel so fragile as if I could collapse at any moment. 'It doesn't feel right all of this,' I say suddenly, 'you just leaving.'

'Come on, Philip,' Michelle says, 'it's time that Doctor Lin went on with his work. I bet he has got loads more people to see and meet.'

'I do indeed. I have to be in Norwich this afternoon.'

'See now, Philip, it's time to rest.'

I shake my head; I don't know if I can rest.

'I'll give you a little something to help you relax'.

He turns to me and smiles. 'Farewell, Mr Goundry. Rest well.'

He leaves and I stare at Michelle.

'How long have I been here?' I suddenly ask.

'Oh, a while now, Philip.' She is plumping up cushions behind me.

'How long?'

'Some time. I can't remember now.'

I shake my head. 'I don't remember.'

'Remember what?'

'Life before, it is like all of what I lived before has vanished.'

'Or it never happened,' she says under her breath.

'What? What did you say?'

'Oh, nothing Philip, you do enjoy winding yourself up. You should be grateful that you have your old memories back, that's what you wanted, all those skeletons out in the open. Dangling there in front of everyone.'

I gulp and cough. Michelle lifts me and I sit up. 'She was taking us, my mother; we were running away. The girl told her about my father; the girl, she told her about Jimmy, about Red and what he was doing to him. She was saving us. I didn't remember until now, she was saving us. Richardson, he was saving us. I didn't remember.' I hold my hand over my mouth. Her orange dress. 'I was only a child. I didn't understand. I thought she was a tiger in the garden; a tiger that was getting closer to the house, that was going to kill us. I shot it, I shot her. I didn't mean to. I didn't mean to.'

'Now,' she says, 'relax Philip, that was all a long time ago.'

'But I killed her.'

'You didn't mean to, you were a child.'

'But ...'

'Hush now, no one needs to ever know this. You're all right, Philip.'

'My father and Red, they were in on it together. Monsters. He wasn't a good man; my father was a monster. Apples don't fall far from the tree; I am a monster.'

'Now don't be saying things like that. You're no monster.

You're a great writer, you're important to so many people. Things happen in our lives that we can't control; you were a child, she was only wanting to protect you, you didn't know it was her. You were only protecting your brother; you did the best you could. Try and rest.'

'I can't.'

'You can, you have earned it. Close your eyes, Philip, it's all coming to an end now anyway.'

I'm exhausted and I look up at her and she pats my hand, she is monitoring my pulse, my breathing becomes slower and I close my eyes. Someone is coming, my mother whispers in my ear. Philip, you better be ready, someone is coming to take us away.

Michelle leaves the room.

I am suddenly scared, something feels wrong, did I miss something?

Tom enters with his clipboard.

A door bangs. I say, 'Someone is coming.'

'Today?'

'Yes. Someone is coming.'

'I don't think so, Philip.'

'No, someone is coming; I can feel it.'

'You haven't had a visitor in months.'

'What are you talking about? Doctor Lin was here, interviewing me.'

He looks at me confused. 'Who?'

'Doctor Lin, from the Singaporean government, he was interviewing me about my childhood.'

He shakes his head. 'No, Philip, there hasn't been any visitors for months. Oh ... hold on. You mean that man that came by last year? Yeah, I remember he was here for a day and then he left.'

'What?'

'Yeah, he interviewed you, but then suddenly you took a turn, it was just before your stroke.' I don't react. 'I remember,' Tom laughs, 'that he ran out of here as fast as his feet could carry him, his face was white as a sheet.' He tucks a blanket around me, 'You don't remember? It's all right if you don't. Short term memory loss is common, still you are doing a lot better, aren't you?'

'I am ... umm. ... I thought he was just here.'

He smiles, 'No, Philip, no one has been here for months.'

A door bangs, a faint cold breeze.

'Someone is coming,' I whisper.

Acknowledgements

This book was inspired by a lecture I attended during my first MSt residence about the role of the unreliable narrator. It is something I would have never ventured to write without the support of my tutors, Sophie Hannah, Jon Appleton, Elly Griffiths, Midge Gillies, and my supervisor Emily Winslow. I thank them all for their encouragement and for inspiring me to explore and experiment with different forms.

I would also like to thank the first readers of this book Liz Jensen, Tom Canning and Ian Ridley, for all their helpful feedback and comments.

To my agents, Jayapriya Vasudevan and Helen Mangham, I am so grateful to you both for everything.

Writing can be a lonely business, but I have been blessed to have some wonderful writing buddies, so thank you Brendan Sweeny, Billy O'Shea, Sophie Morton-Thomas and Anne Mette Lundtofte for all your support. Also, to my MSt cohort at Cambridge, you are all so talented and I'm honoured to be among you.

To the lovely ladies at the National Archives of Singapore, thank you for taking your time with me and for all your assistance.

And lastly to my parents, Ann and Mark, my incredibly wonderful husband Thomas, Haga and my baby girl Cordelia Ann who inspires me every day. I don't know where I would be without you all.

Fiction set in Malaysia

Published by Monsoon Books